ECLIPSE BOUND

BOUND TRILOGY INSTALLMENT

GALAXY ALIEN MAIL ORDER BRIDES
BOOK SEVEN

MICHELLE M. PILLOW

MICHELLEPILLOW.COM

ABOUT THE BOOK

ECLIPSE BOUND

Sci-fi Paranormal Romantic Comedy

Crash first. Kiss later. Save two worlds if there's time.

When a not-so-mysterious flying object slams into Duskrock, Arizona, ex-journalist Rowan Clark expects hype, not a devastatingly calm alien diplomat with starlight eyes and a mission to stop a war.

Eclipse comes from the Twilight Belt of Zorveya, where day and night are locked in endless conflict. He was sent for a discreet cultural exchange, but thanks to the catastrophically inept Galaxy Alien Mail Order Brides, secrecy combusts on impact. When black-ops Milano decides Eclipse and his companions Solar and Lunar belong in cages, diplomacy turns into survival.

On the run with Rowan, Eclipse can't ignore the magnetic pull that breaks every rule. She's done chasing disasters. He's sworn to duty. But in the shadows between danger and desire, their chemistry refuses to stay quiet. To keep Earth out of the crossfire and give his fractured world a chance at peace, Eclipse must decide if love is worth leaving behind everything he holds dear.

--

ECLIPSE BOUND is a steamy sci-fi paranormal romantic comedy with forced proximity, protective alien vibes, a skeptical human heroine, sizzling open-door heat, and a guaranteed HEA.

Book one of the Bound Trilogy installment from the Galaxy Alien Mail Order Brides series.

WELCOME TO QURILIXEN

QURILIXEN WORLD NOVELS

Dragon Lords Series

Barbarian Prince

Perfect Prince

Dark Prince

Warrior Prince

His Highness The Duke

The Stubborn Lord

The Reluctant Lord

The Impatient Lord

The Dragon's Queen

Lords of the Var Series

The Savage King

The Playful Prince
The Bound Prince
The Rogue Prince
The Pirate Prince

Captured by a Dragon-Shifter Series
Determined Prince
Rebellious Prince
Stranded with the Cajun
Hunted by the Dragon
Mischievous Prince
Headstrong Prince

Space Lords Series
His Frost Maiden
His Fire Maiden
His Metal Maiden
His Earth Maiden
His Woodland Maiden

Dynasty Lords Series

Seduction of the Phoenix

Temptation of the Butterfly

To learn more about the Qurilixen World series of books and to stay up to date on the latest book list visit www.MichellePillow.com

AUTHOR UPDATES

To stay informed about when a new book in the
series installments is released, sign up for updates:

michellepillow.com/author-updates

WELCOME TO GALAXY BRIDES

A NOTE FROM THE AUTHOR

Dear Readers,

For those of you familiar with my bestselling series, Dragon Lords, you've already been introduced to the Galaxy Brides Corporation and the services they offer lonely men and women of the future. What you might not have known is that Galaxy Brides (formerly aka "Galaxy Alien Mail Order Brides") dabbled in taking grooms to destinations—namely Earth! Unfortunately, they found the alien males a little too hard to control once they landed on our surface.

I hope you have as much fun reading this series as I've had writing it!

Happy Reading!

Michelle M. Pillow

To My Readers,
For always being willing to take that next adventure
with me.

PLANET OF ZORVEYA

Eclipsyionic stood at the edge of the Twilight Belt, where eternal day met endless night, and wondered, not for the first time, if their world was too fractured to heal. To the west, the gold-tinged brilliance of Solarus City shimmered. The never-setting sun refracted off crystalline spires like the sharpened edges of a weapon. Opposite them, to the east, stood the obsidian towers of Lunaris. They loomed in shadowed elegance, the blackened landscape drinking in perpetual starlight.

And between them, the neutral territory.

The Twilight Belt was a testament to compromise that neither side particularly wanted, but that both grudgingly had accepted. Eclipsyionic lived in the everlasting twilight of his home district and had spent most of his adult years in the Peacemaker Council's diplomatic center, dealing with ambassadors who liked arguing as much as breathing.

Today, he feared that compromise was failing.

Eclipsyionic had believed that if he stood in the middle long enough, he could hold both sides back from the brink. But lately, it felt like he was merely sinking between two tides that refused to retreat.

He was tired of listening to the bickering and had put in for a transfer. Hopefully, with luck, this would be his last time dealing with delegates.

Those in the Twilight Belt long predicted that war was coming between the light and dark. Drastic measures needed to be taken to stop it. The sides needed to find a way to work together.

It was a long shot, but he had tried all the other shots.

"I refuse to dim our towers," Solarestabinian snapped, his golden skin pulsing with suppressed fury. He stalked the conference room, trailing sparks of sun-fueled energy in his wake. "The light is our birthright. Our towers have stood this way for generations."

"Your birthright is blinding half of my sector and giving my people migraines," Luniaren countered from his position in the darkest corner, the hint of his silhouette barely visible against the gloom. His pale skin seemed to absorb what little light reached him, and his darker, night-adapted eyes narrowed. "The new crystal arrays are reflecting directly into Lunaris territory. It's a deliberate provocation."

Eclipsyionic suppressed a sigh. This was the fourth diplomatic incident this month, and it wasn't even halfway through the cycle. It was time to try something truly radical. He touched the data pad containing the latest proposal from Galaxy Alien Mail Order Brides Corporation, an idea so absurd it might actually work where centuries of traditional diplomacy had failed.

Absurd. Ridiculous. Desperate. All apt descriptors. And yet...

"If I may suggest—" Eclipsyionic began.

"You may not," Solarestabinian and Luniaren said in unison, before glaring at each other for agreeing on anything.

A gentle chime from the data pad drew Eclipsyionic's attention. The Galaxy Alien Mail Order Brides' representatives were ready to deliver their proposal.

"Perhaps," Eclipsyionic said carefully, "it is time to consider alternative solutions."

"Such as?" Solarestabinian's golden skin flared brighter with his temper. "More endless talks while they skulk in their shadows plotting against us?"

"We do not skulk," Luniaren said, his voice as cold as the eternal night. "We strategize. Though I wouldn't expect someone who solves everything with brute force to understand the difference. If you had your way, we would be throwing rocks at spaceships and would have lost our mines to the Tyoe. We saved your sparkly asses."

"And if we left it to you, we'd be strategizing how to turn down the Bevlon's hostile takeover from the bowels of one of their lava pits. We saved your inky, spineless—"

A loud beep cut Solarestabinian off as Eclipsyionic activated the data pad's holographic display. A lurid advertisement flashed between the arguing representatives, showing smiling couples of various species embracing beneath a glittering alien logo.

"What," Solarestabinian demanded, scowling, "is this?"

"Galaxy Alien Mail Order Brides," Eclipsyionic explained. "They broker interspecies cultural exchanges."

Luniaren pushed away from his corner, moving

like a liquid shadow to stare at the hologram. "You cannot be serious."

"Their success rate with difficult mating situations is interesting." Eclipsyionic scrolled through several case studies. "They recently succeeded in finding women for ash miners from Bravon—"

Solarestabinian slashed his hand through the hologram. "We're not interested in women who would accept a Bevlon demon into their bed."

"He said Bravon, you stupid wormhole licker," Luniaren snapped.

"Blackhole bait," Solarestabinian countered.

"*And*," Eclipsyionic interrupted, bringing up images of blue aliens next to smaller females, "they paired isolated ice warriors from Sintaz through a series of arranged marriages to Earth humans."

"Earth?" Solarestabinian and Luniaren asked simultaneously, before they resumed glaring at each other.

"A developing planet with no official knowledge of alien life," Eclipsyionic continued, showing images of the blue orb with changing light patterns. "Their society is chaotic, their customs contradictory, and their technological advancement limited. But their capacity for adaptation is remarkable. Plus, they're not unpleasant to behold, as far as alien creatures go."

"And?" Solarestabinian crossed his arms, sun-sparks dancing around his shoulders. Luniaren expanded a shadow toward him like a taunt.

"Their atmosphere, food products, and local terrains are compatible with our kind," Eclipsyionic added. "Implanted nano-translators will take care of the language. Basic customs and information will be provided on the trip."

"And?" Solarestabinian prompted, brightening his body to counteract Luniaren's encroaching darkness.

The hostility was palpable. Eclipsyionic kept a tight hold on his energy, as he fought the urge to explode toward both of them.

"The Peacemaker Council feels that since all other attempts at mediation have been met with resistance, we need to try a new tactic, one where both sides join in an offworld mission." He averted his gaze before clarifying, "A mating expedition."

They look at him like he'd grown another set of arms, but don't speak.

"If representatives from the opposing zones can successfully integrate into Earth society and create relationships with the natives, it would prove that cooperation between contradictory forces is possible." Eclipsyionic tried to hide his exasperation as he looked at them. Being here was like mediating children, not that he had seen children in a long while. There weren't many on the planet outside of the designated spawning centers. "The Galaxy Alien Mail Order Brides corporation is prepared to facilitate this experiment."

"No," Luniaren and Solarestabinian stated in unison.

"One unified goal. A symbolic peace," Eclipsyionic insisted. "If the two of you—"

"Symbolism won't stop a war," Solarestabinian muttered. "This is an absurd proposal."

The two men started bickering again, and Eclipsyionic blocked them out. The council had already signed the contracts. These two were going whether they wanted to or not. He just had to deliver the details.

After sixty cycles of listening to both sides quarrel, he'd finally had enough. Raising his voice, he projected over the arguing. "The Peacemaker Council has decreed it necessary. If you refuse, you will be personally responsible for the council withdrawing our support of—"

"No, wait a moment," Solarestabinian held up his hands, panicked. "There is no reason to be impulsive."

"Says the Solarian." Luniaren's night-dark eyes narrowed further as he returned to the shadows. "What exactly does this decree entail?"

"Do not withdraw support," Solarestabinian insisted. Neither man would want to be responsible for such a thing. They'd be ostracized.

"I'm glad you're both willing to listen to reason," Eclipsyionic said, though he knew better than to believe either of them was truly being reasonable. They were scared of the consequences. He pulled up pictures of the location to show them. "The corporation has arranged for a small compound in a place called Duskrock, Arizona. The planet is not tidal locked like ours, and this area has a good balance of light and dark. Apparently, the locals are quite welcoming of unusual visitors, which will make it easier to blend with the population."

Luniaren and Solarestabinian frowned.

"The idea is simple. You will both travel to Earth and participate in the mating customs," Eclipsyionic said.

"Is our species even biologically compatible?" Luniaren asked doubtfully, though his tone hardly sounded like a question. "They look..."

Luniaren frowned harder, his shadow essence contracting inward.

"I'm told with our energy transformations, you will be able to perform in a way that... pleases..." Eclipsyionic tried to think of a delicate way of explaining what he'd been told, but it was difficult while he was being optically threatened by both sides. "That will pleasurably infuse a mate should it come to such an act."

"Is there no other option?" Solarestabinian insisted. "Can you not arrange a marriage here?"

"Since the few inter-marriages between both sides have proven problematic—" Eclipsyionic began.

"Death is more than problematic," Luniaren interrupted.

"Only one died," Solarestabinian countered.

"Out of three," Luniaren argued. "The others live apart."

Eclipsyionic continued, ignoring them, "You will be working together, living among humans, learning their customs, attempting to find compatible friendships—"

"Friendships? You mean mates." Solarestabinian's golden skin brightened to near-blinding. "With primitives who probably haven't even mastered basic light harvesting?"

"They have something called solar panels that

convert sunlight into energy," Eclipsyionic offered, showing pictures of the panels.

"Primitives," Solarestabinian repeated with disgust.

"A species that adapts rather than evolves. Interesting," Luniaren mused, already calculating possibilities.

"I didn't mean to imply they don't evolve," Eclipsyionic tried to correct. "Just not—"

The two started arguing again.

Eclipsyionic held up his hands. He was about two seconds from throwing them both in a lava pit and calling the mission a failure before it even started. "Whether you find brides is not a concern so much as you work together to complete this mission without harming or abandoning each other, and without alerting Earth authorities to your presence. The Peacemaker Council feels you need a common goal, one not rooted in fighting off planetary attackers on your homeworld. Mutually surviving alien territory is a good first step."

"How far is this Earth?" Solarestabinian interjected.

"How long will this mission last?" Luniaren asked at the same time.

They glared at each other.

"The corporation's representatives will be here shortly to explain the details of your mission." Eclipsyionic checked the time, eager to give the two men over to their new handlers so he could go home. The representatives were late.

As if summoned by his impatience, the conference room's door slid open with a grinding noise and a puff of smoke. Two short, stocky figures stumbled through, coughing and waving away the fumes. Their yellow skin looked pale, like a Solarian left in the dark for too long. Their spacesuits dripped with moisture, and they smelled like the dank waters of the night bogs.

"Apologies about that!" the first one called out cheerfully. His mouth moved, but the words were a few seconds behind the motion. "Slight miscalculation with the transport coordinates. We went to a dark pool. Lovely spot if not for the large creature that ate our trainee Harris. I'm Gary, and this is Bob."

"Blessings from Galactic Acid Melting Your Rides, and organs are strewn in the spaces!" Bob announced, beaming at them. His translator made his words sound crackly.

Gary smacked the back of his long hand against Bob's thigh. "Forgive his damaged translator. He meant to say we're from Galaxy Alien Mail Order Brides, where we join hearts across the universes!"

"We turn women into red soup," Bob added.

Solarestabinian and Luniaren exchanged a look that, for the first time in recorded history, held perfect agreement.

Another puff of smoke clouded the entryway. A third alien appeared next to his coworkers. Green oozed from his cut head, contrasting with the yellow of his skin. Eclipsyionic lowered his head and sighed. This was not going well at all.

"Harris!" Gary greeted, plastering on a strange smile for his customers. "We thought you were dead. Do try to keep up. Death is no excuse to skip out on your first sales meeting."

"Execrates are forthwith," Bob added. "Phalluses rise at the dawning."

Harris tried to speak, but Gary cut him off.

"Harris, give Bob your translator," Gary ordered.

As the two beings exchanged translators, Gary fumbled with a device cobbled together from spare parts. Water dripped from the unit, and he shook it. "Just let me pull up the presentation." He smacked the device against his palm several times until it sputtered to life, projecting a wobbly image onto the nearest wall.

Wearing the new translator, Harris held his injured head. "Pudding."

"As you can see," Bob gestured to what was clearly an upside-down chart, "our success rate is outstanding."

His words were clear, but the tone of his voice projected a few octaves higher.

"That's the failure graph," Gary whispered. "You were supposed to delete that one."

"Ah, yes." Bob quickly turned the device over and changed the screen. "Much better! Now, about our matching process—"

"Your matching process appears to be broken," Solarestabinian interrupted, pointing to the projection where two Killians were attempting to stuff a protesting human female into a suitcase.

"That was an isolated incident," Bob assured them. "We've since implemented strict no-suitcase policies."

"Peccadillos pudding," Harris inserted, not making sense.

"Very strict," Gary added, pushing Harris behind him. "Bob, turn that off. This is the wrong presentation. And we only lost track of those Killians for a few days. Barely even made the Earth news, and all females were recovered and their minds erased. They're fine."

Eclipsyionic felt a pain forming in his head. "Perhaps we should focus on the diplomatic benefits of the—"

"Oh yes!" Bob brightened. "We have an excellent package deal. Three trips to Earth for the price of two, plus complementary skin-suits and internal sound translators for blending in with the local population."

"Three?" Eclipsyionic shook his head in denial. "No. There are only two delegates."

"Skin-suits?" Luniaren's voice dropped dangerously low with disgust. "You want us to look like the Earth humans?"

"Just a precaution," Gary said quickly. "Though the last batch did melt a bit in the sun. We're still working out some kinks, but if that happens, just tell the locals you were disfigured in a vat of acid accident. No problems. Some Earth women like deformed monsters. Just hand those women a book."

"We arranged for two transports," Eclipsyionic insisted, gesturing at his two companions.

Bob and Gary shared a look.

"The signed contract said—" Bob began.

"We are not supposed to say the contract was

already signed." Gary frowned. "They need to think they had a say. Remember, they're delicate beings."

Solarestabinian and Luniaren share a look. No one had ever accused anyone on the planet of Zorveya of being delicate.

"Well, that ship has flown out of the quadrant, am I right?" Bob laughed. He returned to the device and scrolled through more pictures. Eclipsyionic watched as images of various aliens chased terrified Earth women, others proudly held them flailing upside down by their ankles in front of a body of water, and a wormlike creature with a mouth full of razor-sharp teeth tried to bite off a woman's head.

"Look in my direction," Bob ordered.

A device flashed. Solarestabinian sparkled. Luniaren grunted and lifted his arms to block the light.

Eclipsyionic didn't move. He had a bad feeling about this whole situation. This simple assignment was spiraling, and he could feel the edges of control slipping through his fingers like fractured starlight.

"There we are," Gary said, smiling. A photo of Solarestabinian appeared on alien documents. Sparkles shone around his eyes like surprised fireworks. "We have already set up the necessary paperwork so you can assimilate easily into Earth culture. Your human name will be Solar."

"My earned name is Solarestabinian. It means the great warrior of the light guard who fights for the external truth."

"It means wormhole licker," Luniaren muttered under his breath.

"Convenient, right? The Earth humans have a similar name. Solar, of the sun," Gary said. "Very prestigious."

"And popular," Bob added. "Interesting fact, on Earth, you need what they call a surname, a second name belonging to your related family, so you do not mate with a biological replicant. Your surname will be Bound."

"Solar Bound," Gary interjected with excitement. "I picked it myself."

Luniaren smirked. "That sounds accurate."

Eclipsyionic grimaced. Bound was slang for a man caught self-pleasuring in the vine forest.

The image changed to Luniaren's face. His eyes were closed, and his face was scrunched from the harsh flash.

"Meet Lunar Bound," Gary announced.

"No," Luniaren stated.

"Yes," Gary insisted.

"No, I am not family to him," Luniaren's voice hardened in anger. A wave of energy came off him, and the shadows followed him as he aggressively challenged Gary.

"M-moving on," Gary stammered, cowering from the sudden dark cloud looming over him. "Bob?"

"Eclipse Bound," Bob fumbled to change the picture.

Eclipsyionic looked at his face transposed on the Earth documentation in horror. No part of him wanted to go on this trip. "That is not necessary. I will not be traveling to Earth. I—"

"The contract says three," Bob stated. "We're to abduct any who do not go willingly."

"You are the mediator who will report on the trip," Gary said. "Your council was very clear about that. They would not sign the contract otherwise."

"If we must go, you must go," Solarestabinian smirked.

"Yes," Luniaren agreed. "As you said, the fate of our planetary peace depends on it."

This was what these two finally agreed on?

Eclipsyionic looked between the men. A star journey trapped with them?

Perhaps it would be better if he just jumped into a lava pit. It would make for an easier end.

"Wonderful!" Gary beamed. "So it's agreed."

2

ONE EARTH MONTH LATER...

"Have you tried hitting it again?" Bob suggested helpfully from the ship's communication screen.

Eclipse gripped the safety restraints as their vessel shuddered through Earth's atmosphere. The ship's stabilizers had failed twenty minutes ago, shortly after Gary's voice had assured them that minor turbulence was perfectly normal. Now the entire control panel flashed with warnings that Eclipse couldn't read because someone, probably their pilot Harris, had set the display to something other than the star language.

"I do not believe additional hitting will help," Eclipse said through gritted teeth. He sat next to

Harris with Solar and Lunar locked in chairs on opposite sides of the small landing craft.

"Perhaps if you let me—" Solar tried to reach for the controls, trailing sparks of agitation.

"Touch nothing," Lunar snapped from his chair. "Your light energy has already fried half the systems."

"At least I'm trying to help instead of lurking in the shadows like a—"

The ship dropped suddenly, and Eclipse's stomach lurched toward his throat. The communication screen flickered. Bob's yellow face became distorted. Bits of metal rattled around them.

"Not to worry," Bob's chopped voice yelled. "This," the screen went black, "normal... worried," static, "first-time landings."

"Did he say crash landings?" Solar asked.

"First-time landings," Eclipse corrected, though he was beginning to wonder if there was a difference in Galaxy Alien Mail Order Brides' vocabulary.

Harris' communicator had only worked for about five minutes on the trip, not that the trainee seemed to know much about what was going on. He smacked the controller. Alarms started blaring in warning, and smoke curled from the console.

Through the flickering viewscreen, Earth's surface

rushed up to meet them. A cluster of red rock formations loomed ahead, their jagged peaks less than welcoming. Eclipse could make out small structures below, gathered around what appeared to be a circular landing dock.

"Is the ship cloaked?" Eclipse demanded, pushing frantically at the controls. The cloaking indicator light didn't blink.

"That's the yoga retreat we were telling you about with the bendy females," Gary's voice crackled through the speakers. "Try not to destroy too much of it. Earth insurance paperwork is worse than actual murder."

The comms went dead.

"We're coming in too fast," Lunar observed calmly from his shadowed corner. "You should slow the ship."

"Do you think?" Solar's golden skin flared with sarcasm. "I hadn't noticed with all the alarms."

Eclipse ignored them both, focusing on the rapidly approaching ground. The ship's landing dampeners refused to deploy, and the steering controls felt like they were filled with comet dust. Harris kept hitting buttons that made everything worse, including one that triggered a screaming music track to play through the speakers.

"What are the odds we will survive this impact?" Solar yelled over the noise.

"Pudding," Harris declared, his translator still malfunctioning. "We die like brides!"

"We're not brides," Solar shouted.

Eclipse yanked the controls hard to avoid a particularly tall red spire. The ship responded by spinning, giving them all a nauseating view. of ground-sky-ground-sky in rapid succession.

"If we survive," Lunar said calmly, "I really will kill Bob and Gary. Harris will die from his own ineptitude."

"Squish like pizza," Harris answered.

"Not if I get to them first," Solar swore.

Eclipse didn't try to mediate their argument. He was too busy watching a group of humans in strange spacesuits scatter from the docking area below. Most of them had thin, colorful mats rolled under their arms as they ran.

"Remember," Gary announced cheerfully, "the local culture welcomes unusual events. They will think this is entertainment."

"Pudding!" Harris cried out.

The ship clipped a rock formation, and something important-sounding tore away from the hull.

A new alarm joined the chorus. This one sounded distinctly like a countdown.

"Brace for impact!" Eclipse ordered, though it was unnecessary. They'd been braced since entering the atmosphere.

The ship overshot the docking lot like a meteor, bounced once, twice, three times before skidding sideways. Solar's restraints snapped. He slammed into the ceiling, trailing sparks of indignation, before falling against the back of Eclipse's head. Eclipse tried to grab hold of him, but Solar was flung out of his reach.

"Stop glowing," Lunar growled. "You're making the systems worse."

The ship finally ground to a halt, tilted at an awkward angle. The viewing screen remained dark. Solar illuminated a soft light from his place on the floor, allowing him to see more easily. Green smoke filled the ship's interior with a strange smell.

An automated voice announced, "Warning. Atmospheric seal compromised. Emergency protocols initiated."

"What emergency protocols?" Eclipse demanded.

"Beautiful stinkbug?" Harris responded.

The ship creaked, and then, suddenly, their

restraints released and the floor dropped out from under them.

"Pudding!"

3

Rowan stood frozen in the parking lot of the yoga center, watching the distance where the supposed alien spacecraft landed. She'd seen it all in her time working at the retreat. Drones. Strange artifacts found in the desert. Cave drawings. Animal carcasses that were meant to be alien autopsies. People who spray painted themselves green and meeped, *"Meep. Meep. Meep."*

But this? This was...

Someone grabbed her arm. "Did you get it on video?"

Rowan frowned, turning to a woman in bright pink spandex. All around her, sound came rushing back to pull her from her shocked state. When she found that Rowan held a walkie-talkie instead of a camera, the woman moved on to the next closest person.

Rowan walked through the parking lot. Several cars had cracked windshields.

"Was that real? That can't be real." A woman clutched the man next to her.

"The special effects were incredible," someone said in the gathering crowd.

"I'm here! Take me back with you!" a man screamed, running in the direction the ship flew.

"Come on, Rowan," Stephanie, a receptionist, grabbed Rowan by the arm and pulled her toward a jeep. "Let's go find it. You drive!"

"We can't just go over there," Rowan protested, but guests were already hiking into the desert toward the crash site, phones held high. Even Mrs. Henderson, who needed help getting into child's pose, was speed-walking across the parking lot.

A small explosion echoed from the direction of Pete's crystal shop. The crowd cheered. Someone started dancing for social media on their cell phone camera, with smoke in the background.

Rowan lifted her walkie-talkie. "Security? Anyone? We have a situation."

Static crackled back at her. Great. The incident must have interfered with communications.

This was not in her job description. When she took the position at the Duskrock Yoga and Spa Meditation Center, the listing had mentioned *"occasional unusual occurrences"* and *"diverse clientele,"* but she was fairly certain that hadn't included actual UFO crashes. Then again, considering some of the wellness seminars they hosted, maybe that's precisely what they had meant.

"Hey," she yelled after the crowd. "Be careful!"

They were going to be overrun later with cactus thorns, sunburns, and sprained ankles.

"Ro," Stephanie insisted. "Come on. You drive. I film."

"Security, this is Rowan. If you can hear me, you're needed in the parking lot. There was a flyover incident, and we have several guests making a run into the desert headed toward Pete's. Stephanie and I are on our way there now to round them up and facilitate rides back." Rowan hooked the walkie-talkie on her pants and lifted her hand just in time to catch Stephanie's keys. The last thing the retreat needed was a bunch of sun-stroked tourists running around the desert.

As a local, she knew the shortest route to Pete's and it didn't include a desert hike. Stephanie hung out a window, recording with her phone as Rowan cut across a dirt road that looked more like a suggestion than a place to drive.

Wind whipped her hair through the open window. It smelled of burning metal and something weirdly sweet, like caramelized sugar. Dark smoke guided her like a beacon as she pulled up close to Pete's crystal shop. They got out and ran to the front of the gathering tourists. Through gaps in the crowd, she could see Pete beaming with excitement as his business burned.

"I told you they were real," Pete yelled. "They were drawn to the power of the crystals!"

"Pete, your roof is on fire," Rowan pointed out. Firetruck sirens sounded in the distance.

"I know!" He gave a little jump and lowered his voice. "Isn't it magnificent? A real live UFO on my shop. I knew they would come."

Pete had a reason to be excited. In this area, this incident would likely quadruple his sales. But in all honesty, he probably didn't care about the money. Like many around here, Pete was a true believer looking to the stars to confirm his faith.

"Everyone, back up!" A security guard finally showed up, waving his arms. "Clear the area. Make room!"

Rowan helped coordinate the crowd, grateful

someone with actual authority had arrived. However, *authority* might have been overselling it. The security guard was just Ted from the shopping strip's night shift, wearing a wrinkled uniform and strutting around like he was the star of his own reality show. If Rowan had to guess, she would have laid money he'd been napping in his car when the incident happened.

A strange feeling came over her as movement caught her eye. Three men pushed along the edge of the crowd. They stood out because they were heading away from the fire.

The men wore baggy work overalls, but something about them seemed off. The tallest one moved with an unnaturally fluid grace. Another practically glowed. Or maybe he wore some kind of glitter lotion. The third kept his head down and moved along the shadows, like he didn't want to be seen.

The odd coloring on their skin didn't surprise her. Not here. Not when every fifth person in town dressed like life was an outer space cosplay.

It was in the way they moved. Fluid. Graceful. Almost... blurry? She couldn't look away.

"Excuse me, where did you guys come from? Were you by the building? Did you see what happened?" Rowan called out, wanting to slow them down.

The tall one turned, and for a moment, she forgot what she was doing. Something in his expression caused her to stumble. His eyes were dark and caught the light in a way that made them look like stars swam in his vision. He started to come toward her. Her heart beat so hard she felt it in her throat. Before Rowan could process what was happening, Stephanie grabbed her arm and jerked her back to the chaos.

"Ro, look at this footage I got." Stephanie thrust the phone at her.

"No, I..." She muttered, pushing her hand against Stephanie's screen. When Rowan turned back, the three men had vanished into the crowd of UFO enthusiasts.

Rowan spent the next three hours helping to coordinate the commotion. The strange men did not return. She guided retreat guests turned impromptu hikers to cars that would bring them back to the resort, handed out water bottles to overheated tourists, and repeatedly assured everyone that no, she did not have inside information about the alien landing despite working at the retreat.

"It was probably just an experimental aircraft. Pranks happen around here all the time," she kept saying, though she wasn't entirely convinced herself. What she had seen streaking across the sky hadn't looked like any plane or helicopter she recognized.

Then again, in the age of the internet, hoaxes were abundant. Someone probably built a giant drone and recorded the whole thing for likes on social media.

By the time the fire department had Pete's roof under control and the police had cordoned off the area, Rowan's shift had technically come to an end. But as she rode in the back of a pickup to get her car, she still couldn't shake the image of those three strange men walking away from the shop out of her mind.

It wasn't that they were strangers. This was a tourist town, and strangers were everywhere.

It wasn't that their clothes were a little off. Weekends often looked like a comic con. Heck, the guy driving the pickup wore a plastic alien mask and sparkly purple spandex, with a beauty pageant sash that read, *"Abduct me."*

It was his eyes, and the feeling she got in the pit of her stomach when she looked at him.

"Rowan, hey!" Stephanie jogged across the nearly-emptying parking lot, phone permanently clutched in her hand. "Did you see my video got picked up by Channel 12? I've gone viral! Over three thousand new followers."

"Great," Rowan said, fishing her keys from her pocket. She was exhausted and just wanted to go home, make tea, and pretend she had a normal life.

"Look," Stephanie held her phone up to Rowan's face. "I caught them on video. I didn't see it when it happened, but when I was uploading clips there they were!"

Rowan squinted at the screen. The footage was shaky, but she could see four outlines emerging from behind Pete's shop. There, amid the chaos and smoke, were the three men she'd noticed earlier, along with a shorter person, maybe even a child. The child appeared to be giving directions to the other three before disappearing back toward the disaster.

"They came from the crash site," Stephanie whispered dramatically. "I got 'em."

"They're probably just tourists shopping for crystals," Rowan tried to reason. "Everyone was running around. You can't even see their faces."

"No, look." Stephanie zoomed in on the footage. The one on the left is glowing, and the one on the right blends with the shadows when he should have been lit by sunlight.

"It's just lens flare," Rowan said, though she wasn't convinced. "And out of focus."

"Whatever you say, skeptical Sally." Stephanie tucked her phone away. "But I'm telling you, those are not regular dudes. And get this, I've got friends at the Crimson Rock Inn saying three guys matching their description just checked in, paid in cash, and didn't have any luggage."

Rowan rolled her eyes. "So they travel light. Or they left their luggage in the car."

These were not great universal mysteries.

"Or they just crash-landed from another planet," Stephanie countered with a grin. "Anyway, I'm heading to the Crash Zone after I freshen up. Half of Duskrock's going to be there tonight talking about this. You should come."

The Crash Zone was a local bar that catered to UFO enthusiasts and tourists looking for authentic alien encounters. It was tacky, overpriced, and usually full of people wearing tinfoil hats. Literally. Tin foil Tuesday was a thing.

"I'll pass," Rowan said. "We have to work tomorrow."

"Your loss!" Stephanie called over her shoulder as she bounced away. "Text me if you change your mind."

Rowan called herself off shift on the walkie-talkie and drove home to her small rental on the outskirts of town. She'd moved to Duskrock six months ago after her life in Phoenix imploded. Which was a nice way of saying broken engagement, lost job, house fire, anger issues ex. The retreat coordinator position had seemed like a perfect escape, a chance to recalibrate in a place known for healing. No drama. Low risk of a lawsuit.

And until today, it had been getting a little monotonous. She hated to admit that being on the front lines had given her a bit of a familiar rush, and like an adrenaline junkie, it would be so easy to jump right back into her old habits.

In Duskrock, she'd found herself surrounded by crystal healers, chakra aligners, and people who genuinely believed aliens regularly visited Earth to... what? Tune the vibrations of their energy fields? Steal their DNA? Take selfies with the red rocks?

Or her favorite. Probing orifices.

Why were aliens always so fascinated with the anus? She thought that said a lot more about humans than it did about the UFOs.

She pulled into her driveway, noticing her neighbor, Mrs. Lowen, peering through her curtains. The older woman had probably been watching the news about the crash and would corner Rowan for details if she lingered outside for too long.

Inside her house, Rowan kicked off her shoes, put the walkie-talkie on the charger, and headed straight for the shower. She let the hot water wash away the desert dust and lingering smell of smoke, while she tried to convince herself that what she'd seen was just some kind of drone or a publicity stunt for a new sci-fi movie.

But those men...

There had been something about the way they moved, something in their expressions. She couldn't shake it. The tall one had looked at her with such intensity, like he was trying to peer into her soul.

Or maybe she'd read one too many romance novels.

Either way, she felt compelled to deny it, especially to Stephanie, who didn't need more encouragement.

After her shower, wrapped in a comfortable robe, Rowan made herself a cup of chamomile tea and settled onto her small back patio that overlooked the valley. The sun was setting, painting the red rocks in brilliant oranges and purples. This view was what had sold her on the rental, even though it stretched her budget.

Her phone buzzed with a text from Stephanie, *"Aliens at the Crash Zone! Get your ass over here!"*

Attached was a blurry photo of what looked like the back of someone's head at a crowded bar.

Rowan sighed and put down her phone without responding. She was not going to get sucked into Stephanie's alien conspiracy theories. Tomorrow would be busy enough dealing with the aftermath at the retreat, fielding calls from curious tourists, and probably having to issue refunds to guests whose spiritual journeys had been interrupted by falling space debris. Even though they would dine on that story for the rest of their lives, people were people, and they'd use any excuse they could to get a discount.

She was just about to head inside when movement in her peripheral vision made her freeze. Someone lurked in her yard near the fence line where her property met the desert.

"Hello?" she called out, immediately regretting it. If it were an intruder, announcing her presence would not have been the smartest move. Every horror story told her that much.

Silence answered her. Then a soft rustling sound.

Rowan grabbed her phone, ready to call 911,

when a figure stepped into the dim light cast through her window.

It was him. The tall man from earlier.

He stood perfectly still, watching her with those strange, intense eyes. He wore what looked like cutoff yoga pants and a plain t-shirt that was too tight across his shoulders, as if the clothes didn't actually belong to him.

"Can I help you?" Rowan asked, her voice steadier than she felt. There came that adrenaline rush again, teasing her senses, begging her to run forward when she should back away.

The man tilted his head slightly, studying her. When he finally spoke, his voice was surprisingly melodic, with an accent she couldn't place. "I have come to speak to an authority."

Rowan frowned.

He touched the side of his neck. "Is my translator malfunctioning? Can you understand my words?"

She wasn't sure how to answer that. "Uh, yes, I understand you."

"You saw us."

It wasn't a question.

"I saw a lot of people today," Rowan replied carefully. "It was chaotic."

"Yes." He nodded, as if pleased with her answer.

His arms twitched like they were trying to get out of his skin. His delusions could be running very deep. She needed to be careful.

"Chaos is an effective camouflage," he said. "It allowed us to walk amongst the locals."

Okay, so he was a weirdo. Or on drugs. Possibly both. Rowan's fingers hovered over her phone screen.

"Look, sir, I don't know what you want, but you're trespassing on private property," she said firmly. "You can't be here."

"I apologize for the intrusion." He stepped closer, and Rowan again noticed something odd about his movements. They were too fluid, like he glided rather than walked. "I am Eclipse. I need your assistance."

"Eclipse?" Rowan frowned. "Is that your actual name?"

I mean, sure. It was possible. One of the pool girls at the retreat was named Cosmos.

"Eclipsyionic. But Eclipse Bound is the name I have been assigned for this mission," he replied, completely serious. "Bound is the surname."

She took in a steadying breath. This man was deep in his roleplay.

"Right. Well, Eclipse, unless your mission is to get arrested for trespassing, I suggest you leave."

Rowan tried to appear more confident than she felt. "Now."

He stopped advancing but didn't retreat. "I have no wish to be taken by Earth militants. But I must speak with you. You work at the facility where we were to arrive. You have access."

"Access to what? The yoga retreat?" Rowan laughed despite her nervousness. "Anyone can book a class online."

"We require accommodation that will not draw attention," he continued as if she hadn't spoken. "The dwelling provided by Galaxy Alien Mail Order Brides has proven inadequate."

Rowan blinked. "Galaxy Alien... what now?"

She frowned and looked around the lawn to see if someone was hiding. She felt eyes on her, but couldn't detect anyone. Was this Stephanie trying to pull a prank?

Eclipse sighed. "The corporation responsible for our transit to this location. They have placed us in a structure that does not offer sufficient separation between Solar and Lunar. I fear they may destroy each other before our visit can properly begin."

"Stephanie? Is this you?" Rowan called. "Very funny."

"No. My name is Eclipse," he answered. "Eclipse Bound. Bound is a surname."

"So you're not happy with your tour group package?" Rowan asked, finally unlocking her phone.

"No. The travel was a death trap, and they have abandoned us," he answered. "I watched you organize the people. You are the contact authority we need to talk to."

"Okay, I think you need help that I can't provide," she said, deciding to call the police. "I'm going to call someone who—"

In a movement too fast to track, Eclipse was suddenly beside her, taking the phone from her hand.

"Please," he said quietly. "I do not wish to cause alarm. But I must ensure the success of this mission. The peace of my world depends on it. I have been watching you. Your energies are not like the others here."

Up close, Rowan noticed that his skin had a strange, subtle shimmer to it, not quite golden like his friend from earlier, but not normal either. And his eyes weren't any color she'd seen before, somewhere between dusk and twilight.

"Your... world," she repeated slowly.

Eclipse nodded.

"You expect me to believe that you're from..." She couldn't look away from his eyes. Were they contacts? Why were tiny stars moving in his gaze like he contained a galaxy inside his head? She slowly pointed toward the sky.

"Zorveya. We are not from your planet. I believe that is now obvious."

Rowan stared at him for a long moment. Then she started to laugh. She couldn't help it. The stress of the day, the absurdity of this conversation, it was all too much.

"Of course you're not," she said between laughs. "You're aliens. Why not? This is Duskrock, after all. We get all types here."

Eclipse frowned, clearly not understanding her reaction. "Your skepticism is understandable but inconvenient."

"Look, Mr. Bound," Rowan composed herself. "I've had a very long day. I had to deal with a lot of overexcited tourists. I'm tired. I probably have a touch of heat stroke. So if you could just give me back my phone and leave, I'd appreciate it."

"The device." Eclipse looked down at the phone in his hand as if just remembering he'd taken it. He handed it back to her carefully. "I apologize for the intrusion. But I must insist that you consider my request."

Rowan glanced down at her phone and noticed it was fully charged. That wasn't right. Her battery had been at eleven percent.

"Which is what, exactly? To help you find a new hotel because your friends don't get along?"

"Essentially, yes," Eclipse replied with complete seriousness. "The Crimson Rock structure has a room that is too containing. Solar requires light. Lunar requires darkness. I require them not to kill each other before our diplomatic mission can be completed."

Rowan rubbed her temples, feeling a headache coming on. "And this mission is...?"

"To find suitable Earth mates and demonstrate that cooperation between opposing factions is possible."

"Mates?" Rowan choked. "Like breeding partners? Strippers? Prostitutes?"

Why was she entertaining this conversation? Maybe she was the one who needed a doctor. Severe dehydration could cause hallucinations.

"Yeah, I don't work for that kind of hotel," Rowan said. "I wouldn't even know how to procure a hooker for you and your friends. Maybe you should try Nevada where it's legal."

Eclipse's expression shifted slightly, almost embarrassed. "No, we do not wish to hook a female. We are not Bevlon. The corporation refers to them as brides, though I find the term reductive. The goal is to form meaningful connections with compatible humans to prove that vastly different beings can coexist harmoniously. It is not mandatory that we succeed in that task, but it is mandatory that we try as a unit. I believe this may all be a test and they are monitoring our progress."

"I see." Rowan didn't see at all. "And let me guess, I'm supposed to be one of these compatible humans?"

"That was not my intention in coming here," Eclipse said quickly. "Though my matching algorithm did identify you as a potential candidate."

"The matching algorithm," Rowan repeated flatly. He sounded like what she imagined AI would sound like if it tried to take human form.

"Yes. When you approached us in the crowd, your biorhythms registered as harmony-compatible with my own." Eclipse stated this as if it were the most normal thing in the world. "But that is secondary to our immediate shelter needs."

Rowan took a deep breath. This guy was clearly

delusional, possibly dangerous, but also oddly compelling. And if he was staying at the Crimson Rock Inn with two other guys who couldn't stand each other, well, she could understand wanting different accommodations. That place was notorious for its paper-thin walls.

"Okay, Eclipse, here's what I can do," she said finally. "I can give you the names of a few vacation rentals that might have availability. Places where your friends can have some space from each other. But that's it. I'm not getting involved in whatever roleplay scenario you've got going on."

"Roleplay?" Eclipse looked genuinely confused. He tapped under his ear. "I do not think that is translating correctly."

"You know, pretending to be aliens looking for wives." Rowan waved her hand dismissively. "It's fine, Duskrock attracts all kinds. No judgment. But I'm not interested in being part of it."

Eclipse stood very still for a moment. Then he reached into his pocket and pulled out a small, metallic object. The patio light appeared to get sucked inside, as if it drew power from the light source.

"Perhaps this will help clarify matters," he said, pressing the object between his fingers.

It hummed to life, projecting a three-dimensional image into the air between them. A detailed map of stars and planets rotated before centering on an orb with distinct light and dark hemispheres.

"This is Zorveya," Eclipse explained. "My home. Currently on the brink of civil war between the light and shadow zones. Our mission here is not a roleplay. It is a last-ditch effort to prove that coexistence is possible."

Rowan stared at the hologram, her mind racing. She reached her hand into the image. It moved around her fingers, undisturbed. Her hand tingled as if electricity flowed into her. This wasn't a trick of light or some app on a smartphone. The projection had depth, detail, and moved in ways that defied logic.

"This isn't real," she whispered, but her conviction was wavering. She touched the object in his hand, careful not to brush his skin. It wasn't metal. It felt like dipping her finger into oil. She jerked her hand back. Her finger remained clean.

"I assure you it is," Eclipse said quietly. "And now, I must ask for your discretion as well as your help. For both our worlds' sake."

Rowan looked at Eclipse's face. There was no deception she could detect. Just a weary determination. But then how would she know what deception looked like in an alien?

"I must return to prevent Solar and Lunar from destroying the accommodations," Eclipse said, deactivating the device.

The hologram vanished, leaving Rowan blinking in the sudden dimness. The porch light brightened behind her.

"But I will come back tomorrow. Perhaps by then, you will have considered my request." He reached into his pocket and pulled out a wad of cash, pushing it into her hand. His fingers swept over hers, and she felt an electrical jolt. "Here, for the shelter. We have more currency if you require it."

Before Rowan could respond, Eclipse stepped back into the shadows at the edge of her yard and seemed to simply fade from view. One moment he was there, the next gone, with no sound of retreating footsteps.

Rowan stood frozen on her patio for several seconds before being propelled into action. She rushed inside, locked every door and window, and poured herself something stronger than tea. As she sipped her emergency whiskey, she picked up her phone and stared at Stephanie's message.

After a long moment, she typed a reply, *"I don't think that's them."*

4

EARTH WAS WORSE THAN PROMISED.

And Galaxy Alien Mail Order Brides was beyond incompetent. This had to be part of the test. They told them they're here to mate, but then crash-land them into chaos, abandon them, and see how they fare. They could only hope that the corporation would come back and this situation wasn't permanent.

Eclipse slipped back into the Crimson Rock Inn through a service entrance, carefully avoiding the cameras he'd identified earlier. The Earth security systems were primitive but numerous, and maintaining a low profile was essential to the mission.

Someone should have given him a heads up.

Someone should have told him he was going on this assignment.

Someone should have explained how to talk to the females.

Rowan Clark.

The Earth overlord system made it easy to access her name. People walked around connected to it, feeding it a constant stream of information.

He reached into his pocket for his energy stone. It tapped into their internet system easily and brought up a series of images of his target. These Earth humans were bending creatures, twisting themselves into odd positions, which was strange considering they didn't walk with much grace.

When they arrived at Crimson Rock, it had been daylight. Then twilight. Now darkness. That would take some getting used to, watching the elements flow together like that on the same location. Thankfully the sun wasn't as bright here, and there was only the one, so Lunar was able to manage, though he'd been miserable.

Light came from under the door as he neared their room. He found Solar inside sitting cross-legged on the floor of their shared suite, his golden skin pulsing with light as he absorbed energy from the desk lamp he'd dismantled and rewired. Now it was his turn to look miserable.

The furniture had been rearranged into what appeared to be defensive formations, and scorch marks decorated one wall.

"Where have you been?" Solar demanded without looking up. His fingers were tracing patterns in the air, trailing sparkles of light. "Lunar has been skulking around the perimeter for hours. I think he's planning something."

"He's patrolling in the dark," Eclipse corrected, surveying the damage to their accommodations. "Where is he now?"

"How would I know?" Solar snapped. "He disappears into shadows."

Eclipse sighed. "We've been on Earth for less than twelve hours, and you've already damaged our dwelling."

"It wasn't me," Solar protested. "Lunar tried to darken the room by covering the windows with those fabric hangings, and they caught fire when I was merely trying to maintain adequate light levels."

"Merely trying?" Lunar's voice drifted from a corner that should have been empty. The shadows seemed to coalesce, forming his tall, slender silhouette. "You deliberately increased your output when I entered."

"Perhaps I was simply happy to see you," Solar said with a dangerous smile.

A wave of darkness grew from Lunar, trying to snuff out the lamp.

"Enough," Eclipse interrupted. "This behavior is precisely why the council sent us here. If you cannot manage to share a dwelling without destroying it, how do you expect our people to share a planet?"

"The council has exiled us," Solar complained. "And your corporation has abandoned us."

"It is not *my* corporation. I didn't hire them," Eclipse said. "I'm trapped here same as you. Our only hope is to prove to them we're capable of working together so they bring us home."

Both aliens had the grace to look chastened, in their own ways. Solar dimmed slightly, while Lunar stepped further from the shadows and stopped trying to snuff out the lamp.

"The human living arrangements are unacceptable," Lunar said after a moment. "This structure offers no proper darkness, except for the waste receptacle, and he," he jabbed a finger toward Solar, "refuses to moderate his emissions."

"I have found a potential alternative," Eclipse

said. "I've made contact with a local human who may be able to assist us."

"You revealed yourself to an Earthling?" Solar's light flared with alarm. "We were supposed to blend in."

"I revealed enough," Eclipse replied carefully. The truth was, he hadn't planned on telling her everything he did, but when he heard her voice, he felt he could trust her. "She works at the arrival site. Her name is Rowan Clark."

"The one who approached us in the crowd," Lunar observed quietly. "She saw too much."

"She did not report us to the authorities or put us on the planet's overlord system." Eclipse didn't bother asking how Lunar knew which human he'd spoken to. The shadow-dweller's observation skills were unmatched. It was possible he followed Eclipse there.

Solar inched closer to his lamplight. "You sound soft when you say her name."

"Yes, I admit, her biorhythm scan shows compatibility markers," Eclipse said. "And she responded with skepticism rather than fear. That's a promising sign."

"Compatibility?" Solar smirked, his golden skin brightening with amusement. "Eclipse, are you developing an interest in the human mating aspect of our mission?"

"I am focused on diplomacy," Eclipse said stiffly. "My personal preferences are irrelevant."

"Of course," Lunar murmured, a hint of knowing in his night-dark eyes.

"The corporation's representatives are still missing," Eclipse changed the subject. "Their communication silence is concerning."

"Concerning, but not surprising," Solar snorted. "They couldn't navigate a straight path through open space."

"The human overlord network indicates unusual activity near our landing site," Lunar said, holding up a primitive Earth device. "They call this device a phone. I've been monitoring their information streams."

Eclipse examined the device Lunar offered. The screen displayed what appeared to be a social platform filled with blurry images of their crash and wild speculation about aliens. He sent his energy into the device to move around the various parts of the internet viewing port. An Earthman's face appeared as if the device belonged to him.

Eclipse pulled the energy stone from his pocket. "As have I."

"The authorities say we are a publicity stunt," Lunar continued, taking the device back. "Or a weather balloon. Or something called swamp gas emissions. Their theories are creative. Apparently, there is also something called mass hysteria on this planet. One person has a thought, and it spreads like a disease."

"Good," Eclipse said. "Confusion and competing narratives will work in our favor. However, you should dispose of that device. Humans appear very attached to them, and I am sure the owner will come looking."

Lunar kept hold of it but nodded.

"Speaking of confusion," Solar interjected, "what exactly is this?" He held up a small paper card that read "Continental Breakfast, 6-9AM. Lobby Level."

"I believe it's an invitation to a feeding ritual," Eclipse said, remembering the information packet Galaxy Alien Mail Order Brides had provided. "Humans require regular nutrient intake."

"As do we," Lunar pointed out. "The corporation promised that compatible sustenance would be available."

"There's a vending machine down the hall," Solar said. "I examined it earlier. It contains packages of various substances, but requires small metal discs to operate."

"We have currency," Eclipse reminded them, pulling out one of the packets of "cash" they'd been given. "We should attempt to blend in by participating in their morning feeding. Perhaps you can find a mate there."

"And then?" Lunar asked.

"Then we wait for Rowan," Eclipse said. "She will either help us or not, but we must be prepared for either outcome. Our mission objectives remain clear. We must attempt to find compatible humans, demonstrate cooperative behavior, and not alert Earth authorities to our true nature."

"Simple," Solar said dryly.

"Impossible," Lunar corrected.

Eclipse looked between them, wondering if they realized how similar they sounded despite their differences. Most of the time, he believed they argued just to be contrary.

"Get some rest," he told them. "Tomorrow we begin our Earth adaptation in earnest."

"I'm not tired. The light is finally bearable," Lunar said.

"Try," Eclipse ordered.

His companions retreated to their respective

corners. Solar stayed in the lamplight. Lunar draped a blanket over the furniture and crawled underneath. Eclipse sat on the edge of the uncomfortable human sleeping platform and removed the energy stone from his pocket.

He activated the holographic projector with a touch, keeping the illumination low to avoid disturbing the tenuous peace. The image of Zorveya appeared, spinning slowly in the air before him. He zoomed in on the Twilight Belt, the narrow strip of habitable land between eternal day and endless night where he'd spent his life maintaining the balance.

Eclipse stared at it for a long time, wondering if he was doing the right thing. The Peacemaker Council had given him this mission as his last assignment, but he couldn't help feeling there was more to their decision than they'd revealed.

With a sigh, he deactivated the projector and lay back on the bed, his mind still filled with the image of Rowan's startled face when she'd reached into the hologram. She'd been frightened, yes, but also curious.

If only he could be certain she wouldn't report them to Earth authorities, and blow any chance they had at getting home.

5

Rowan had almost convinced herself that last night had been a dream.

Almost.

The whiskey glass still sat on her coffee table where she'd left it, and her phone showed the text to Stephanie, simple evidence that something had happened. Not to mention the wad of cash he'd pressed into her hand. But holograms? Aliens? A man named Eclipse with stars in his eyes?

Everything she could write off, but not those eyes.

"Get a grip," she muttered, pouring coffee into her travel mug. She resisted adding a splash of whiskey to combat her slight hangover.

She had a full schedule at the retreat today.

There were damage control meetings about the incident. Three yoga classes needed rescheduling. Plus, she had a call with the insurance company about Pete's roof because the resort owned the property, and her bosses didn't want to deal with it. These were normal, practical problems that required normal, practical solutions.

Not alien diplomacy.

Aliens.

The word sounded insane. Well, more so than usual.

She checked her reflection in the hall mirror. Dark circles shadowed her eyes, but otherwise, she looked like her usual self with sensible clothes and hair pulled back in a no-nonsense ponytail. She was the kind of woman who dealt with reality, not interplanetary matchmaking schemes.

Her phone buzzed with an incoming text from Stephanie, *"You missed all the fun. Aliens showed up. I made out with one of them."*

Rowan rolled her eyes.

"Or he might be a cowboy from Kansas City," came a follow-up text along with the picture of a naked man's ass. The cowboy was passed out on a bed. *"I'll ask him when he wakes up. Cover for me?"*

"Can't. Get to work. Today will be crazy," Rowan answered.

"Boo!"

Rowan tossed her phone into her bag, grabbed her coffee, and headed out the door.

The drive to Duskrock Yoga and Spa Meditation Center took her past Crimson Rock Inn. Without thinking, she slowed down as she passed and scanned the parking lot and windows. What was she expecting to see? Three aliens hanging out by the pool with mimosas?

"This is ridiculous," she told herself, accelerating again. "I've been living here too long. I had heat stroke from too many hours spent helping guests in the desert sun."

It was more likely than an alien asking her for help after crash landing on Earth.

But as she pulled into the retreat's parking lot, she couldn't shake the nagging feeling that Eclipse would indeed return as promised. And worse yet, she couldn't deny the tiny flutter of excitement that accompanied the thought.

The retreat was buzzing with activity when she arrived. A news van from Channel 12 had parked by the entrance, and a cluster of tourists with cameras stood near the meditation garden, pointing toward the distant crash site. The van reminded her of her past life, and she felt that tiny rush of excitement that came from chasing a story. She forced her eyes to turn away. That wasn't her job anymore.

Before Rowan was out of her car, Darren, the retreat manager, waved frantically from the entrance.

"Rowan. Thank goodness. The insurance adjuster is here, and Channel 12 wants a statement about yesterday's incident. And Mrs. Craine is demanding a refund because her energy vortex is disturbed, even though she received all the services she paid for."

"I'll be right there," Rowan called back, stopping to scan the crowd for her mystery man. He was nowhere to be seen.

The morning passed in a blur. Rowan filled out paperwork, drafted a carefully worded statement for the company blog about unusual atmospheric phenomena, and placated disgruntled yoga practitioners with promises of free aura cleansings. Though, really, what did they expect? UFOs were a part of the local culture. It hardly seemed worthy of complaint. On the opposite side of that spectrum, the hint of UFOs and visitors from outer space was good for booking rooms to capacity. The front desk had become a sea of telephone rings.

"Who is this Eclipse group you have booked in the Desert VIP suite?" Stephanie asked as Rowan tried to sneak away to her office. "There is no information in the company profile or billing info, and no services are listed."

"Alien enthusiasts. I didn't have time to fill it out. They paid me in cash. I'll do it later. Just leave it booked," Rowan answered. "I'm going to be hiding in my office."

"You got it, boss." Stephanie gave a small salute.

Her office looked like a cookie-cutter of every other office at the retreat. It had the same lamp, the same pastel desert landscape painting, and the same tan office chair, as if the owners had received bulk discounts on all things blah.

Rowan leaned over and dug into her secret candy stash in the back of her bottom drawer. Her office door opened without someone knocking.

She frowned and dropped her candy bar. "Just a—"

Eclipse filled her doorway. He wore jeans and a button-up shirt that almost fit properly, but there was no mistaking those otherworldly eyes. He clutched a bag in his hand.

Rowan pushed to her feet, glad the desk was

between them. Her heart beat quickened. "How did you get in here?"

Her hands shook nervously as she glanced at the hall behind him.

Eclipse closed the door with deliberate care and then stepped toward her with fluid grace.

"Rowan Clark," he said, her name like a soft melody in his strange accent.

"Seriously, how did you get back here?"

"Your security is minimal," Eclipse replied.

"They let you wander around?"

"The human male at the entrance was very helpful when I told him I was here for you." Eclipse remained between her and the door, keeping a respectful distance. "Have you considered my request?"

In the better lighting, she saw a strange tint to his skin, almost a purplish-blue undertone.

"This can't be happening," she whispered. "How are you doing that with your eyes? They look like stars."

Eclipse took a single step forward.

"You recharged my phone by touching it." She looked at his hands. They seemed mostly normal, but for the color. "This isn't real."

"I am very real," he assured her, reaching to touch her arm. "Feel."

Rowan swallowed hard. "Just because you're real in the sense you're not a hallucination doesn't mean I believe you're an alien diplomat on a mission to find Earth brides."

Even as she said it, she felt energy humming off his skin, traveling into her arm. Her stomach tightened in response.

"What would convince you?" he asked, tilting his head.

"I don't know," Rowan said. She leaned closer to him, drawn into the humming. The vibrations reached all the way to her toes, but that wasn't the particular body part she concentrated on.

"I accept," he stated.

"Accept?" She felt breathless. Her nipples ached. Her legs felt weak. All from the single touch of his vibrating hand.

"Yes." He suddenly jerked her forward so that her body pressed into his. The entire length of him was pure energy. It washed through her in one giant pulse.

Eclipse gave a strange moan that sounded as if someone strangled him. He stepped forward, pushing her back until she came up against a wall.

He rocked his hips forward to pin her body before focusing on her breasts. The sounds he made became louder as he grabbed two handfuls and squeezed. Another pulse of humming energy hit her like a giant vibrator.

Instinct dictated that she lift her leg to give him access, but as her thigh traveled upward, he squeezed her breasts tighter and began to shake. They hadn't even removed their clothing. It left her in a mix of pleasure and frustration. She wanted to tear his clothes and have him fill her, but an orgasm hit her surprisingly hard.

"You have favorable energy," he said in approval. His hands stayed gripped on her breasts. "And I quite enjoy these portals."

"I..." She couldn't think of how to respond. Her heart beat fast and hard. This couldn't be real.

The lights in her office flickered wildly. Eclipse instantly stepped away from her and put distance between them. The computer monitor came to life, surged, and then died.

"What's—?"

Before she could get the question out, her door opened again, and Eclipse's friend strode in, trailing actual sparks from his fingertips. His skin had a golden sheen that pulsed with each step.

"Eclipse, come. We have a problem," he announced, ignoring Rowan completely. "Lunar is skulking, and I believe he's tracking a human female."

"You're glowing," Rowan whispered, eyes wide.

The alien finally noticed her. "I see you have located your woman with the compatible biorhythms." He circled Rowan, studying her with unnerving intensity. "She seems adequate."

"Solar," Eclipse warned. "We discussed proper Earth protocols."

"Yes, yes. Don't call humans inadequate to their faces. I remember. I said she is adequate." Solar waved dismissively, causing the lights to flicker again. "But we have more pressing issues. Lunar is displaying signs of possible mate fixation on a loud female, and if he follows his instincts, he may—"

"He wouldn't harm her," Eclipse interrupted.

"Of course not," Solar looked offended. "But he might be attempting communication, which would be far worse. You know how he gets. All shadows and cryptic statements. Humans find it unsettling. I have seen references in their horror movies. They will try to exercise him."

"Exercise?" Rowan looked between them, her skepticism evaporating with each passing second. "I think you mean exorcise."

"Yes." The golden shimmer of Solar's skin couldn't be makeup, and the way the electronics responded to his presence defied explanation.

"You really are aliens," she said faintly.

Solar turned to her with a brilliant smile that was literally so dazzling that she had to shield her eyes. "Of course we are. Did Eclipse not explain properly? Galaxy Alien Mail Order Brides sent us to your primitive planet to find mates and prevent an interplanetary war. Though why anyone would want to mate with a species that can't even regulate their own bioelectricity is beyond me. No offense."

"Solar," Eclipse said sharply. "Find Lunar. Now. Before he causes a diplomatic incident."

Solar gave a mock salute and started to leave.

"Wait," Rowan demanded. "You can't keep walking around the retreat like that. I have a suite put aside for you. It's private."

"Find him and then find the suite. Stay out of sight," Eclipse said.

Solar left with spark trails that faded before touching the floor.

Alone again with Eclipse, Rowan found herself at a loss for words. The evidence of her eyes contradicted everything she thought she knew about reality.

And if that wouldn't have been enough, the lingering feeling inside her body was.

"Are you alright?" Eclipse asked, his voice gentler than before.

"I don't know," she answered. "I think I'm having an existential crisis."

"That is a common response to first contact scenarios," he said. "Your cognitive framework is adapting to new information."

"That's one way to put it." Rowan ran a hand through her hair, dislodging her neat ponytail. "So let me get this straight. You three are from a planet called..."

"Zorveya."

"Right. And you're here because your planet is divided between light and shadow people who hate each other, and somehow finding human wives will fix that?"

Eclipse winced slightly. "That is an oversimplification, but essentially correct. Solar represents the Solarus Zone, Lunar the Lunaris Zone, and I am from the Twilight Belt. We were chosen as representatives for a diplomatic experiment."

"To prove that if three very different aliens can peacefully exist on Earth and find love, your warring factions might be able to coexist?" Rowan summarized.

"Yes," Eclipse looked impressed. "You understand quickly. I had feared it would be more difficult for the human mind to reason."

"And this Galaxy Alien Mail Order Brides?"

Eclipse sighed. "Yes. They abandoned us. They are the only corporation with the necessary permits for this type of cultural exchange. Their competence is questionable."

Rowan laughed despite herself. "That's putting it mildly if they crashed you into Pete's crystal shop."

Eclipse's expression softened at her laugh, and for a moment, Rowan felt a connection growing between them.

The moment was broken by screams from the hallway, followed by the sound of breaking glass.

"That would be Solar finding Lunar," Eclipse said with resignation. He held out his hand to Rowan. "Will you help us? Before they destroy your retreat as they did our accommodations?"

Rowan hesitated for only a second before taking his hand. It was still warm, with a subtle vibration that tingled up her arm. It instantly made her want to press against him again.

"I must be insane," she muttered. "But yes, I'll help you."

Eclipse's fingers tightened around hers. "Thank you, Rowan Clark. Your assistance may save two worlds."

"Let's start by saving the retreat," she replied, pulling him toward the door. No part of her wanted to fill out more insurance paperwork. UFO invasion wasn't covered under their plan. "Then we can worry about interplanetary diplomacy."

As they hurried down the hallway toward the commotion, Rowan couldn't help noticing that Eclipse hadn't let go of her hand. And strangest of all, she didn't want him to.

6

ECLIPSE FOUGHT TO REMAIN NEUTRAL AS HE watched Solar and Lunar retreat to their respective rooms. After they caused a commotion at the retreat's dining area, he had managed to convince both of them to come to the suite before their energy signatures drew even more unwanted attention. Thankfully, the staff dining area had been empty at the time, and only Rowan and the woman Lunar had been following saw them.

During Solar's interruption in Rowan's office, he had observed subtle changes in his companion. Solar's golden essence pulsed with unfamiliar patterns that suggested some kind of emotional engagement, though Eclipse could only speculate. He mentioned a fire dancing female in passing, which seemed like it would interest the light-dweller. More surprising was Lunar's shadow form, which had been intensified when they found him confronting the female he'd been skulking after. For Lunar to show interest in any being was unprecedented.

Now they were safely contained again, at least temporarily. Solar's room was bright and sunny. Lunar's embraced the dark. The suite Rowan had secured was remarkably suitable, with distinct zones that accommodated their biological needs while maintaining proximity. A diplomatic solution worthy of the Peacemaker Council.

If only the council could see them now. Three aliens hidden in a luxury suite on Earth, each already forming connections with human females despite their protests otherwise.

"The mission parameters did not anticipate this," Eclipse muttered to himself, moving to the central living area. The space was balanced between light and shadow, much like his home in the Twilight Belt. A rare comfort since arriving on this planet.

He removed the increasingly uncomfortable skin-suit, allowing his natural form to emerge. His skin had a subtle purple-blue luminescence, neither as bright as Solar's golden glow nor as light-absorbing as

Lunar's shadow form. Evolution had adapted those in the Twilight Belt to exist between extremes, to mediate, to find balance.

To be forever caught in the middle.

It was exhausting. More and more, he just wanted to tell both sides to throw themselves into a dark swamp for all eternity.

The energy stone he kept in his pocket projected Zorveya's image into the air before him. A wave of unexpected homesickness came over him. Rotating the projection, he focused on the narrow habitable strip between day and night where he'd spent his life walking political tightropes.

"Display mission parameters," he instructed. The stone responded, replacing the planet image with scrolling text.

"*Mission Objective: Demonstrate peaceful coexistence and cooperative potential between representatives of Solarus and Lunaris zones through successful integration on Earth.*

"*Duration: Minimum one Earth month.*

"*Success Metrics: 1. Formation of meaningful connections with compatible humans. 2. Absence of conflict resulting in property damage or exposure. 3. Unified return to Zorveya.*

"*Failure Conditions: 1. Mission abandonment by*

any participant. 2. Exposure of alien origins to Earth authorities. 3. Irreparable conflict between representatives."

Eclipse deactivated the projection with a sigh. Less than forty-eight Earth hours into their mission, and they'd already caused property damage at two separate locations and revealed their true nature to humans. If the council received a full report, they would likely extend their exile indefinitely.

He wondered what the odds were of Galaxy Alien Mail Order Brides actually monitoring them. It's not like they were running a superior operation. After the crash landing and hasty directions, they'd all but abandoned them.

Perhaps that had been the intention all along. Remove three influential voices from the political equation before hostilities escalated.

A soft knock on the suite's door interrupted his thoughts. Eclipse quickly reapplied his skin-suit before answering, finding Rowan on the threshold. Her presence stirred an unexpected response, a resonance in his energy field that hadn't diminished since their last meeting.

"I brought supplies," she said, holding up several bags. "Food, clothing that might fit better, and some local guidebooks."

"Thank you." Eclipse stepped aside to let her enter. "Your assistance is appreciated."

Rowan moved into the common area, setting her bags on a table. "Is everyone settling in?"

"They have claimed their territories," Eclipse answered. "Solar has the eastern room, and Lunar the western. The arrangement should minimize conflict."

"That's good. I made sure to erase the security videos. There's no evidence of you moving around the retreat." She began unpacking items, organizing them with efficient movements. "I brought some blackout curtains for the western room and full-spectrum lights for the eastern. I thought they might help."

Eclipse studied her, noting the care with which she'd selected items specifically suited to their needs. "You're being extraordinarily accommodating to three aliens who crashed into your life."

Rowan paused, a small smile forming. "Would you believe this isn't the strangest thing that's happened since I started working here?"

"What could possibly be stranger than extraterrestrial visitors?"

"Last month, a guru convinced twelve people to bury themselves up to their necks in the desert overnight to commune with the earth. We had to rescue them from flash floods." She shrugged. "Duskrock attracts a certain type."

"Including us," Eclipse observed.

"Including you." Her eyes met his, and that resonance intensified. "Though I suspect you didn't choose this destination."

"No. Our travel arrangements were made by Galaxy Alien Mail Order Brides."

"Right." Rowan resumed unpacking. "The interstellar dating agency. Still processing that thing exists."

Eclipse moved beside her, helping to arrange the items. "Our Peacemaker Council engaged their services as a last-ditch diplomatic effort. The concept is that if representatives from opposing factions can peacefully integrate on a neutral planet and form connections with natives, perhaps cooperation is possible back home."

"And the service abandoned you here? After crashing your ship?"

"Their representatives are less than competent," Eclipse admitted. "But they claim to be securing the ship and retrieving our supplies."

Rowan looked skeptical.

"I believe we must adapt to our circumstances regardless of their reliability."

She nodded, seemingly satisfied with his answer. A comfortable silence fell between them as they continued unpacking. Eclipse found himself surprisingly content in her presence, her biorhythms harmonizing with his own in ways that defied logical explanation.

"So," she gave him a once-over, "what do three single aliens do on a night like this?"

"Solar's going to a place called Crash Zone to see a fire dancer, and Lunar is meeting that woman, Poppy, from the dining room later to explore some caves."

Rowan raised an eyebrow. "For a group supposedly focused on diplomatic missions and finding shelter, you all moved pretty fast on the dating front."

"They would deny any romantic intentions," Eclipse said. "Solar claims he's researching Earth combat techniques, and Lunar is investigating Poppy's unusual perceptive abilities."

"Uh-huh." Rowan's expression suggested amused disbelief. "And what's your excuse?"

The directness of her question caught Eclipse off guard. "I don't have a romantic agenda. My role is to mediate and report on the success of this diplomatic experiment."

"Right. That's why your hands were all over me

in my office earlier today." Her cheeks flushed slightly at the memory. "What was that about, anyway? One minute we were talking, and the next you were... *vibrating*."

Eclipse felt an unfamiliar sensation. Humans might call it embarrassment? "I apologize for my impulsive behavior. Physical contact with compatible biorhythms can trigger unexpected energy transfers. I should have maintained better control."

"I'm not complaining," Rowan said, her voice softening. "Just trying to understand. On Earth, we generally don't get to second base within minutes of confirming someone's an alien."

"Second base?"

"Never mind." She waved dismissively. "The point is, I felt something when you touched me. Like energy flowing through my entire body. That's not normal for human contact."

Eclipse considered his response carefully. "My people can share energy through physical connection. It's an intimacy usually reserved for established bonds."

"So you basically alien-kissed me without buying me dinner first."

Despite her teasing tone, Eclipse sensed genuine curiosity beneath her words. "The resonance between us is unusual in its intensity. I've never experienced such immediate compatibility."

Rowan's expression shifted, becoming more serious. "Is that why you trusted me so quickly? Because of this biorhythm thing?"

"Partly," Eclipse admitted. "But also because of your actions. You've helped us without seeking advantage, provided accommodations suited to our needs, and kept our presence concealed from authorities. These are not the behaviors of someone with harmful intent."

"I could just be setting you up for government capture," she pointed out.

"Are you?"

"No." Her immediate response carried conviction. "But you can't just trust everyone you meet here, Eclipse. I'd speculate that Earth isn't like your diplomatic zones. People lie. They manipulate. They exploit differences."

"That is not unlike our zones," he said quietly. "Shadows and light, forever suspicious of each other's motives."

Rowan seemed to consider this. "Maybe that's why I'm helping you. I know what it's like to be caught between opposing sides, trying to maintain balance."

Eclipse sensed there was more to her statement, a personal history she wasn't yet sharing. Before he could inquire further, sounds of movement came from the eastern room.

Solar emerged, wearing new Earth garments that strained against his muscular frame. His skin-suit was visibly deteriorating, golden light leaking around the edges.

"These coverings you bought me are inadequate, Eclipse," Solar complained, tugging at the shirt. "And this skin-suit is failing. I cannot maintain human appearance much longer."

"I brought alternatives," Rowan said, retrieving a bag she hadn't yet unpacked. "These might work better. They're made for desert sun protection. Looser fit, better coverage."

Solar examined the offerings with skepticism but accepted them with a nod that, for him, constituted gratitude. "I must prepare for my research expedition to The Crash Zone to learn combat techniques."

"Research," Eclipse repeated dryly. "Of course."

Solar ignored his tone. "When will the corporation representatives arrive with our real supplies? The communication device has been silent."

"They said they would contact us when the ship

is secured," Eclipse replied. "I wouldn't anticipate immediate assistance."

Solar muttered something uncomplimentary in their native language before retreating to his room with the new garments.

"Is he a warrior?" Rowan asked once Solar had gone. "I can tell he's all light and fire."

Eclipse nodded. "From the Solarus Zone. The light-dweller society values strength, direct action, and visible display. Subtlety is not their strength."

"And the other one? Lunar? He's all shadow and stealth?"

"The Lunaris Zone had to evolve differently to their environment to survive. Shadow-dwellers value observation, strategic patience, and the conservation of resources. Living in perpetual darkness creates different priorities."

Rowan absorbed this information. "And you? What does the Twilight Belt value?"

"Balance," Eclipse answered simply. "We exist between extremes, facilitating communication, finding compromise, maintaining equilibrium."

"That sounds exhausting."

Eclipse hadn't expected her perception. "It can be. Constantly mediating between sides that fundamentally mistrust each other takes its toll."

"Is that why you agreed to this mission? To escape the pressure?"

The question struck closer to the truth than Eclipse was comfortable admitting. "I was selected by the council because of my diplomatic record."

"That's not an answer." Rowan's gaze was steady, penetrating.

"No," he conceded. "It's not."

Another silence fell. Eclipse found himself wanting to share his true circumstances. He'd submitted a transfer request due to his growing disillusionment with the endless, circular negotiations. He also had a suspicion that this mission was less about peace and more about removing problematic voices from the political equation.

But such admissions might compromise the mission further.

Before he could decide, the western door opened, and Lunar emerged from the shadows. Unlike Solar, he moved with fluid grace, his form barely visible as he kept to the darker portions of the room.

"I require sustenance," Lunar stated. "The local provisions at Crimson Rock were inadequate for shadow metabolisms."

Rowan gestured to one of the bags. "There's food in the kitchen area. I included options for different dietary needs." She hesitated. "Though I wasn't entirely sure what aliens eat."

"We generally process energy rather than matter," Lunar explained. "But certain organic compounds can be converted more efficiently than others. Dark plants, fungal matter, fermented substances."

"So mushrooms, dark greens, and wine?" Rowan translated.

Lunar inclined his head slightly, which Eclipse recognized as approval. "Acceptable substitutes."

"Check the second bag," Rowan suggested. "I included several local specialties that might work."

As Lunar investigated the provisions, Eclipse noted the ease with which Rowan adapted to them. Most humans would struggle to comprehend, let alone accommodate, three aliens with radically different biological needs.

"You're remarkably calm about all this," he observed quietly.

Rowan shrugged. "I've always been good in a crisis. It's the everyday stuff I struggle with." Something in her expression suggested deeper meaning, but she quickly shifted focus. "Besides, if I freak out about aliens, I'll never hear the end of it from Stephanie."

"The loud female from the crash landing," Lunar identified from across the room. "She took recordings of our arrival."

"Yes, and she's convinced you're here to either abduct her or enlighten humanity," Rowan said with a hint of exasperation.

"I have watched her short movies on your overlord devices," Lunar continued. "She does not appear to be a being of logic."

"Overlord...?" Rowan dismissed the comment with a small sound. "Yeah, well, please avoid her if possible. She can't keep a secret."

"Noted," Eclipse agreed. "We should minimize contact with humans beyond those already aware of our nature."

"Speaking of which," Lunar interjected, "Poppy has invited me to observe nocturnal wildlife at a nature preserve tonight. Her knowledge of shadow-adapted Earth species may provide useful comparative data."

"Is that what we're calling dating now?" Rowan murmured, just loud enough for Eclipse to hear. "Comparative data collection?"

Eclipse suppressed his amusement. "Just maintain your cover identity and avoid drawing attention."

"Unlike Solar, I do not cause electrical disruptions with my mere presence," Lunar pointed out. "My shadow-walking remains effective despite the skin-suit limitations."

After selecting several items from the food supplies, Lunar retreated back to his room without further comment.

"He's cheerful," Rowan remarked once he'd gone. "Though he's not wrong about Solar. He appeared as a flickering, bright spot on the security cameras. Lunar was barely detectable."

"For Lunar, that conversation was practically effusive," Eclipse replied. "Shadow-dwellers are not known for social niceties."

"Unlike twilight diplomats?" There was that teasing tone again, accompanied by a smile that created unexpected resonance patterns in Eclipse's energy field.

"We have our moments of directness," he said, moving slightly closer to her. "When circumstances warrant."

Rowan's pulse quickened, a reaction Eclipse could perceive even through his dampened senses. "And what circumstances would those be?"

"Compatible biorhythms," he answered, allowing a controlled pulse of energy to emanate from his form. "Mutual curiosity. Shared objectives."

"And what are our shared objectives, exactly?" Her voice had lowered, creating an intimacy in the space between them. Her energy called to him like a beacon. He couldn't ignore its pull. He felt himself drifting toward her.

Eclipse considered the question carefully. The mission parameters specified that they were to form meaningful connections with compatible humans. But his interest in Rowan transcended mission requirements. There was something about her energy signature, her directness, her ability to balance practical concerns with acceptance of the extraordinary.

"Understanding," he said finally. "Of each other. Of the possibilities between different worlds."

Rowan studied him, her expression thoughtful. "You know, on Earth, when someone's interested in someone else, they usually just ask them to dinner."

"Would you like to have dinner with me, Rowan?"

His quick response seemed to surprise her, but her smile widened. "Yes, I would. But maybe not in the suite with your roommates lurking."

"We do not lurk," Lunar yelled from the other room.

"I know a location," Eclipse offered, "with a

viewing platform overlooking the valley. We could observe your planet's sunset while consuming nutrients."

Rowan laughed. "When you put it like that, how can I refuse?" She checked the time on her communication device. "I need to finish some work at the retreat first. Meet me at the main entrance in two hours?"

"I will be there," Eclipse confirmed.

After Rowan departed, Eclipse remained in the central space, processing the interaction. He had initiated a social ritual with a human female. A *date* according to Earth terminology. This aligned with mission parameters, yet felt surprisingly personal.

The energy stone in his pocket suddenly seemed heavier, a reminder of the report he would eventually need to file. How would he describe these developments to the council? Three representatives of a divided world formed connections with Earth females within days of their arrival. Would they believe the timeline happened so fast? He was sure Lunar could calculate the odds to that question, but he didn't want to hear them.

Perhaps there was hope for their diplomatic experiment after all. If they could find common ground with an entirely different species, might they not eventually do the same with each other?

If they succeeded, the council would have to let them return home, regardless of any secret agendas.

Eclipse moved to the window, watching as the sun began its descent toward the horizon. Earth's day-night cycle created a constant transition, much like the perpetual twilight of his home. But here, both sides experienced darkness, both knew light. Perhaps that made all the difference.

In two hours, he would join Rowan for the dinner ritual. But, for the time being, he had reports to update and two volatile companions to monitor. The diplomat's work was never done, even on a distant world with unfamiliar stars.

But for the first time since arriving on Earth, perhaps for the first time in longer than he cared to admit, Eclipse found himself looking forward to what came next.

7

Sunset in Duskrock was unlike anything on Zorveya.

As Eclipse waited for Rowan outside the retreat's main entrance, he found himself transfixed by the spectacle. The red rocks caught the fading light, their hues deepening from terracotta to crimson before glowing with an almost internal fire. The sky above transformed through gradients of blue, gold, and magenta in a cycle that Eclipse's people never experienced.

"Beautiful, isn't it?" Rowan's voice broke his reverie.

Eclipse turned to find her approaching, having changed from her work attire into a simple dress that complemented the twilight colors around them. The sight of her created a resonance in his energy field that had become increasingly familiar yet no less intense.

"Yes," he agreed, not specifying whether he meant the sunset or her appearance. "The transitional phases of your planetary rotation create remarkable effects."

Rowan smiled. "Only you could make sunset sound like a scientific observation and a compliment at the same time."

"It was meant as both," Eclipse clarified. He offered his arm in a gesture he'd observed humans performing. "Shall we proceed to the nutrient consumption location?"

Her laugh was warm as she slipped her arm through his. "You mean dinner? Yes, let's go."

They walked to her vehicle, a modest transportation device she called a compact SUV. Eclipse had studied the mechanics of Earth conveyances during their journey, but experiencing one first-hand was a different matter. The interior smelled faintly of the coffee the hotel had kept offering him.

"I am curious. I smell the coffee everywhere. Do humans require this beverage to live?" He located a lidded cup in the console as the source.

Rowan laughed. "I can't speak for all humans, but I practically live on it."

Small crystals and foliage hung from the mirror, and what appeared to be fossilized plant matter was secured to the dashboard.

"And this?" He gestured at the objects.

"Desert sage for cleansing energy," she pointed at the mirror before moving her finger down to the dashboard, "and a piece of petrified wood. It's supposed to be grounding. A gift from a client who thought I needed to be more rooted."

"And did it root you?" Eclipse asked.

Rowan's smile turned wistful as she started the engine. "Possibly. I've moved around a lot. Never stayed anywhere long enough to put down roots. But this place feels promising."

As they drove away from the retreat, Eclipse observed how she handled the vehicle with easy confidence, navigating the winding roads with practiced precision. The sunset continued its spectacular display, painting the landscape in ever-changing hues.

"I've arranged for us to have dinner at a place called Luciérnaga," Rowan said. "It's on a ridge with a good view, relatively private, and the food is excellent. I thought you might appreciate the panorama."

"You have considered my preferences with remarkable accuracy," Eclipse noted. "Just as you did with the accommodations for Solar and Lunar."

"I'm good at reading people," she replied with a shrug. "Part of my job. Though I admit, aliens are a new challenge."

They drove in comfortable silence for several minutes, ascending higher into the red rock landscape. Eclipse found himself studying Rowan's profile, the way the fading light played across her features, the subtle energy patterns that radiated from her physical form.

"You're staring," she said without taking her eyes off the road.

"I am observing," Eclipse corrected. "Your biorhythms have unique harmonic patterns. They create resonance fields that interact with my own energy in ways I had not previously experienced."

Rowan glanced at him briefly, her expression amused. "Is that your scientific way of saying you find me attractive?"

"Attraction is an inadequate term for the phenomenon," Eclipse replied. "I do not think humans have the perfect words to explain it. But yes, it encompasses part of the experience."

They arrived at the restaurant, a structure of

glass and stone that seemed to emerge organically from the red rock cliffside. Inside, a host greeted them and led them to a table on the patio overlooking the valley, where the last rays of sunlight illuminated the landscape in gold.

"Ms. Clark, we have your requested table," the host said with practiced courtesy. "Your server will be with you shortly."

Once they were seated, Eclipse took in the panoramic view. "This location provides optimal observation of both geological formations and atmospheric conditions."

Rowan smiled as she unfolded her napkin. "And the food's pretty good too."

A server approached with water and recited a list of fermented grape beverages Eclipse recognized as alcohol. Rowan selected something called a cabernet, then helped Eclipse navigate the menu, explaining various Earth food preparations and ingredients.

"I recommend the grilled vegetables and perhaps the fish," she suggested. "Based on what you told me about your dietary needs, those might align best with your metabolism."

When the server departed with their selections, Eclipse found himself studying the other humans in the restaurant. They seemed oblivious to his non-

Earth origins, accepting his presence without question despite his slightly unusual appearance.

"Your skin-suit is holding," Rowan noted when she found him studying his arm. "Though it's thinning around the eyes. And the star-like quality of your gaze is noticeable."

"Does it concern you?" Eclipse asked.

"No," she answered honestly. "I find it beautiful. But we should be careful. Others might start to notice."

Their wine arrived, and Rowan demonstrated the ritual of tasting before acceptance. Eclipse followed her example, finding the liquid complex and not unpleasant, though it created unusual energy patterns in his system that would require monitoring.

"So," Rowan said after they'd both sampled the beverage, "diplomatic mission aside, why are you really here, Eclipse?"

The directness of her question caught him off guard. "The mission parameters were as I explained."

"Yes, I know the official story," she said, leaning forward slightly. "Three aliens sent to Earth to prove different kinds can get along by finding human mates. But there's more to it, isn't there? I can see it in your eyes when you talk about your world."

Eclipse considered his response carefully. The

mission was classified, yet Rowan had already demonstrated both trustworthiness and remarkable perception.

"The situation on Zorveya is more complex than I initially conveyed," he admitted. "The tensions between the Solarus and Lunaris zones have escalated beyond diplomatic solutions. War is imminent. That will leave us vulnerable to outside attack. Other aliens who want to harvest minerals will likely return and attempt to take over again. We'll be weakened, and they will succeed. My world will be wiped out within five Earth years."

"And sending you three away is supposed to help how?" Rowan asked, skepticism evident in her tone.

"Officially, our success would demonstrate that cooperation is possible between the sides when we have a shared purpose," Eclipse explained. "There is a misperception on my planet that the sides cannot be around each other due to varying energy signatures, and that too long of an exposure period causes sickness. I think it's an excuse not to try, rather than an actual genetic phenomenon. However, I suspect our selection was strategic for other reasons. Solar is a high-ranking member of the Solarus Elite Guard. Lunar has connections to the Shadow Intelligence Network. Both would be influential voices in any military conflict. If we convince them that they can work together, it'll make them advise their people toward peace instead of war. Hatred runs deep. There are those who would rather die than compromise."

"And you?"

"I had submitted a transfer request from the diplomatic corps," Eclipse admitted. "After sixty cycles of mediating the same arguments with diminishing results, I had become disillusioned. I think my being sent here is a punishment for leaving."

He was surprised he admitted it out loud.

Rowan's expression softened with understanding. "With you gone, they think they can have more control over the situation."

"That is my assessment, yes." Eclipse took another sip of wine, noting how the liquid blurred the edges of his energy containment. "The Peacemaker Council framed this as our last hope for peace, but I believe they may have already decided conflict is inevitable."

Their food arrived, momentarily pausing the conversation. Eclipse examined the grilled vegetables and fish with curiosity before attempting to mimic Rowan's use of the metal implements.

"So you're political exiles," Rowan summarized after the server departed.

"In effect, though not officially," Eclipse agreed. "Galaxy Alien Mail Order Brides was contracted as a convenient mechanism for our removal. Their incompetence was likely an unanticipated factor."

Rowan laughed softly, though there was little humor in it. "Exiled to Earth through an interstellar dating service. That's a new one."

"And yet, despite the circumstances, I find this exile increasingly acceptable," Eclipse said, meeting her gaze.

A slight flush colored Rowan's cheeks. "Because of our compatible biorhythms?"

"That is part of it," Eclipse acknowledged. "But there is more. Your world has variables we lack on Zorveya. The cycling of light and dark. The adaptation to change. The acceptance of differences." He gestured toward the now-darkened landscape, where lights from the town below created a mirror of the stars above. "Solar and Lunar experience both day and night here. On our world, they never would. Unless the other side took them prisoner."

Rowan seemed to consider this as she ate. After a moment, she asked, "Do you think they sent you here hoping you'd never return?"

"The possibility exists," Eclipse admitted. "Though I believe they anticipated our eventual repatriation, chastened and marginalized by our failed mission."

"But what if the mission doesn't fail?" Rowan challenged. "What if you actually succeed in proving different kinds can coexist?"

Eclipse's expression turned thoughtful. "That would create a significant political complication for those advocating war."

"Which means you three and your human connections might be in danger if you actually accomplish what you were sent to do," Rowan concluded.

He didn't like to think that his presence in her life would put her in danger.

They continued to talk, the conversation moving easily between them. The implications hung unspoken as they continued their meal. Eclipse found himself appreciating not just the harmonic resonance of Rowan's energy field, but the quick precision of her mind. She grasped political complexities without the benefit of knowing Zorveyan history or culture.

"Your insight is remarkable," he noted. "Have you had experience with political exile?"

Something flickered in Rowan's expression, but was quickly concealed. "Not exactly, but I understand what it's like when systems turn against individuals."

"You have personal experience with this," Eclipse observed.

Rowan took a longer sip of wine before responding. "I used to be a journalist. Investigative reporting for a major newspaper in Phoenix."

"This is no longer your profession," Eclipse stated rather than asked.

"No." Rowan carefully set down her glass. "My last big story was an exposé on corporate corruption. A company called Milano Enterprises was diverting funds from its charitable foundation to finance some questionable research. I had sources, documentation, everything needed for a solid story."

Eclipse noted how her energy patterns shifted as she spoke, creating dissonance that suggested emotional distress despite her controlled tone.

"The story never ran," she continued. "My editor killed it. Then I was reassigned to cover society events. When I pushed back, I was fired. My sources disappeared or recanted. The documentation I'd gathered vanished from my locked desk. The only good thing about it was a breakup with a non-supportive boyfriend."

"This Milano enterprise retaliated against you," Eclipse concluded.

"Within a month, I'd lost my job, my reputation, and my apartment burned down under suspicious circumstances that could never quite be proven as arson." Rowan's voice remained steady, but her hand tightened around her wine glass. "I got the message. So I left Phoenix and came here, where my college roommate helped me get the job at the retreat."

"You were exiled for revealing the truth," Eclipse said.

"Truth is dangerous to people with power and secrets," Rowan said with a small smile that didn't reach her eyes. "Sound familiar?"

The parallel to his own situation was unmistakable. "Indeed."

Their conversation paused as the server cleared their plates and offered a selection of desserts. Rowan selected something called chocolate lava cake for them to share, explaining it was mandatory for first dates on Earth.

As they waited for the dessert to arrive, Eclipse noticed a shift in the energy patterns of the restaurant. A new presence entered the space, creating subtle disruptions in the ambient field. His gaze moved to the entrance, where a man in a dark suit spoke to the host while scanning the dining room.

"What is it?" Rowan asked, noticing his sudden alertness.

"We are being observed," Eclipse said quietly. "The male at the entrance is actively searching for someone, and his energy pattern suggests purpose rather than casual interest. I have seen him before around you."

Rowan glanced over, her expression changing as she recognized the man. "That's James Petersen. He works for Milano Enterprises' PR department."

"The corporation you investigated," Eclipse said.

"Yes, and he shouldn't be in Duskrock." Rowan's voice remained calm, but her energy flared with alarm. "This can't be a coincidence."

The man spotted them, his gaze locking on Rowan before shifting to Eclipse with narrowed eyes. He said something to the host and began moving in their direction.

"We should leave," Rowan said, already reaching for her purse.

Eclipse calculated their options. The patio had a secondary exit that led to a viewing platform, but the man would likely intercept them before they could reach it. Confrontation seemed inevitable.

"Ms. Clark," the man said as he reached their table, his tone professionally cordial, though his energy pattern registered hostility. "What a surprise finding you here."

"Mr. Petersen," Rowan acknowledged with equally false politeness. "I didn't realize Milano had business in Duskrock."

"Recent developments have expanded our interests in the area," he replied, his gaze shifting to Eclipse. "And you must be the companion Ms. Clark has been seen with today. James Petersen, Milano Enterprises." He extended his hand.

Eclipse recognized the Earth greeting custom and responded appropriately, careful to modulate his energy output to avoid any unusual sensations during the contact. "Eclipse Bound."

"Unusual name," Petersen observed.

"I am not from this region," Eclipse replied truthfully.

"Clearly." Petersen's smile didn't reach his eyes. "In fact, there's been some interesting satellite data from yesterday around Duskrock. Unusual atmospheric disturbances, electromagnetic anomalies. The kind of thing that interests certain departments at Milano."

Eclipse maintained a neutral expression, but internally, he assessed the threat level of this interaction. The man's knowledge was indirect but pointed, suggesting organized surveillance rather than a chance encounter.

"Sounds like material for another one of Milano's questionable research projects," Rowan said, her voice cool.

Petersen's smile tightened. "Always the investigative reporter. But I thought you'd learned that some stories are better left unpursued, Ms. Clark."

"Is that a threat, Mr. Petersen?" Rowan asked directly.

"Not at all. Just friendly advice." He turned his attention back to Eclipse, and he fixed his gaze on the alien's eyes for a long time. "Mr. Bound, you might want to be careful about the company you keep. Ms. Clark has a history of finding trouble."

"I find her company most enlightening," Eclipse replied.

"I'm sure." Petersen placed a business card on the table. "When you're ready for a more productive conversation about yesterday's events, give me a call.

Milano Enterprises rewards those who provide valuable information."

With that, he nodded and departed, leaving the card on the table like a small weapon.

Rowan released the breath she'd been holding. "That was not good."

She picked up the card and tore it in half before dropping it into her water glass.

"They are aware of our arrival," Eclipse confirmed. "Though their information appears incomplete."

"Milano has resources," Rowan warned. "If they're investigating the crash, they won't stop with satellite data."

Their dessert arrived, the server oblivious to the tension at the table. The chocolate confection released heat and scent that would normally have intrigued Eclipse, but his focus remained on the new threat.

"You should not be associated with me if it places you in danger," Eclipse said once they were alone again.

Rowan's expression hardened. "I've been looking over my shoulder for six months. I'm not about to start running again because James Petersen showed up at dinner."

"Your safety—"

"Is my concern," she interrupted firmly. "And frankly, I'd rather face Milano with aliens on my side than alone."

Eclipse studied her, noting the determination in her energy pattern despite the fear beneath it. "You are remarkably resilient, Rowan Clark."

"Necessity," she replied with a small shrug. "Now eat your lava cake before it gets cold. We shouldn't let Milano ruin a perfectly good first date."

Despite the lingering tension, Eclipse found himself appreciating her defiance. She pushed the dessert toward him, demonstrating how to break the cake to release the molten center.

Eclipse tried the sweet confection and choked.

Rowan suppressed a smile. "Not good?"

"It is fine," he managed. "I wish to complete this first date ritual to your satisfaction."

Eclipse reached to take another bite, bracing himself for the horrible test of will this dessert would take.

Rowan reached for his arm to stop him. She shook her head in denial and slid the plate in front of her. "You do not have to eat it."

"Are you sure? I wish for you to be happy with

this date. I will not make you eat this test of wills alone."

"But I like chocolate." She grinned and took a big bite. "Simply means I don't have to share. More for me."

He took the wine to mask the taste of the molten lava. It made no sense that humans would enjoy eating such a thing.

Eclipse considered the new variables in their situation. Milano Enterprises was clearly a potential threat, one with both resources and motivation to investigate the crash. Their interest in him and his connection to Rowan created additional complications.

And yet, as he watched Rowan deliberately enjoying the chocolate despite the encounter, he found himself unwilling to sever their connection. The resonance between them had already grown beyond mere biorhythmic compatibility. There was a shared understanding and a parallel in their situations that created deeper meaning.

He felt a deep stirring inside of his core, like bound energy about to explode. His essence wanted to flow into her as it had in her office. Before Solar interrupted them, he had felt her human body responding unusually to his touch, and he wanted to know more. None of his curiosity was about missions or scientific exploration.

He wanted to physically envelope Rowan.

"We will need to warn Solar and Lunar of this threat," she noted as she finished the dessert.

"Let's give them until tomorrow," Eclipse said, thinking more about what it would feel like to exchange energy with her without the hindrance of her clothing. "They know to be on high alert. Let them have tonight on their dates."

"You're probably right. I doubt Milano will make a move tonight," she said after some consideration. "That was Petersen feeling out the situation. Though we should remain alert and assume they're trying to keep tabs on us."

Eclipse nodded, but he wasn't really thinking of her words, as he wondered how best to communicate his desire to touch her portals and absorb into her.

8

After paying for the meal, a process Eclipse found needlessly complex compared to Zorveyan resource exchange systems, they left the restaurant by the main exit, both watching for any sign of Petersen. The parking area appeared clear, but Eclipse maintained heightened awareness as they walked to Rowan's vehicle.

The night had fully claimed the sky, and stars were brilliant above the red rock silhouettes. As Rowan drove them back toward the retreat, Eclipse found himself trying not to stare at the heat signature he found between her legs. A couple of times, he started to reach for it, but forced his essence to retract into his form.

Instead, he tried to compare Earth's constellations to the star patterns visible from the Twilight Belt. They were different arrangements, yet were equally beautiful in their complexity.

"Where to now?" Rowan asked as they approached the retreat. "Back to the suite? I imagine Solar and Lunar won't be there."

"That is likely," Eclipse agreed. "Solar's interest in the fire manipulator was evident, and Lunar appeared to have formed a connection with Poppy despite his denials."

Rowan drove in silence for a moment, her fingers tapping thoughtfully on the steering wheel.

"We could go to my place," she suggested finally. "It's not far from here, and we'd have privacy to discuss what to do about Milano."

The invitation carried implications beyond strategic planning, and both of them knew it. Eclipse considered the many variables. There was the increasing deterioration of his skin-suit, the potential risk to Rowan if they were observed together, and the growing resonance between them that made proximity both desirable and distracting.

"That would be acceptable," he decided against his better judgment.

He saw the heat between her thighs rising in temperature. Unable to help himself, he let a tiny trail of his essence drift toward her. As he made the smallest of contact, she gave a light gasp and sat up straighter.

The heat drew him in, pulling more of his essence into her body like a vacuum needing to be filled. He slipped into a wet crevice, and she gasped louder. The vehicle swerved as she pulled to the side and hit the brakes.

Her hips wiggled and her mouth opened wider as she drew in a shaky breath. "Easy there, tiger."

"I am not a tiger," he said. "And this would be easier if you remove your coverings."

"Stop for a moment," she breathed heavily. "I can't drive when you do that. We'll wreck."

He reluctantly obeyed and withdrew.

Rowan smiled as she resumed driving. She turned onto a side road that wound through stands of juniper and prickly pear. "Fair warning, I'm not sure how clean it is. I wasn't planning on company."

"Clean is a subjective assessment," Eclipse noted. "I find your presence alters my perception of physical locations."

"That might be the sweetest thing anyone's ever said to me," Rowan replied, her energy field brightening with genuine pleasure. "Even if it does sound like something from a physics textbook."

They arrived at her home, and she stopped the vehicle in front. She lived in a small cluster of homes surrounded by nature.

Rowan kept her eyes carefully forward. "Try not to make eye contact with Mrs. Lowen. She's my nosy neighbor, currently looking through her curtains at us. Once she starts talking, she doesn't stop."

Eclipse nodded, understanding the directive. He dared one glance at Mrs. Lowen. Her forehead pressed against the glass of her dwelling as she stared at them. He refocused his attention on Rowan's door as they quickly walked up the drive.

Inside, the space reflected her practical nature while revealing aspects of her personality Eclipse hadn't yet observed. Bookshelves lined one wall, filled with volumes on journalism, politics, Earth history, and surprisingly, astronomy. Plants occupied sunny corners, their energy signatures indicating that they had been carefully tended. A desk held a computer and neatly organized files, while a comfortable-looking sofa faced both the fireplace and the large window with its panoramic view of the valley in front of the house.

"Nothing fancy," Rowan said, setting down her keys. "But it's mine, and it has a good view."

"It is well-suited to its purpose," Eclipse observed.

He wanted to resume touching her where they left off in the SUV, but she had told him to stop, and he would respect that. "And reveals much about its occupant."

Rowan raised an eyebrow and studied him. Her cheeks were still flushed from what he'd done in the car. After a moment, she cleared her throat and went to the kitchen area. "Oh? And what does my home reveal about me?"

"You value knowledge," Eclipse said, gesturing to the books. "You seek to nurture life, despite your transient history," he indicated the plants. "And you appreciate the balance between practical function and aesthetic pleasure." He nodded toward the furniture arrangement that maximized both comfort and the view.

"Not bad," Rowan acknowledged. "Would you like tea? It's a human custom after dinner. It doesn't taste like the chocolate."

"I would like to experience this custom," Eclipse agreed, though he would much rather experience touching her.

As Rowan prepared the tea, Eclipse examined the photographs displayed on a small side table. Most showed landscapes rather than people, though one featured a younger Rowan with an older woman who shared some of her features.

"My grandmother," Rowan explained, noticing his interest. "She raised me after my parents died. She's the one who taught me to question everything and never take the official story at face value."

"A valuable perspective for a truth-seeker," Eclipse noted.

"It was," Rowan agreed, a shadow passing across her expression. "She died while I was in college. Cancer. Sometimes I think it's good she didn't live to see what happened with my career. She was so proud when I got an internship at a newspaper."

Eclipse sensed the complex emotions behind her words. "I believe she would be proud of your resilience, regardless of external circumstances."

Rowan looked up from the tea she was preparing, something vulnerable briefly visible in her expression. "Maybe. She always said character shows most clearly when everything else is stripped away."

The kettle whistled, breaking the moment. Rowan poured hot water into two mugs, adding leaves contained in small perforated metal spheres. The herbal aroma that rose with the steam was not unpleasant.

They moved to the sofa, mugs in hand. Through

the window, the night sky spread before them, stars brilliant in the clear desert air.

"Tell me about your stars," Rowan requested, settling beside him. The tease of her nearness drew his energy toward her in what humans would call a slow seduction.

Still, he waited for permission to touch her again. He saw the flush in her cheeks and the heat in her thighs.

"The star patterns visible from the Twilight Belt are unique," Eclipse confirmed. "The perpetual dusk creates conditions for continuous observation without the cycling that occurs on Earth."

He described the major formations visible from his home, using his energy stone to create small holographic representations in the space between them.

Rowan watched with fascination as miniature stars formed patterns. She reached out to pass her fingers through the tiny lights. "It must be beautiful where you're from, always seeing the best part of the day. Do you miss it?"

"Those in the Twilight Belt have always been defined by our position between extremes," Eclipse said. "I knew my place."

"It sounds exhausting," Rowan observed, not for the first time. "Always being the one in the middle, always trying to keep the peace between opposing sides."

"It can be, particularly when both sides resist compromise. But there is more to it than diplomatic peacekeeping. Our art, our science, our culture all express this fundamental aspect of our existence. There are clear lines. I miss the familiarity of it. The simplicity. Earth is full of contradictions. Your lines blur and twist like your changing sky. I find it very confusing."

"You requested a transfer. There must be something different you were looking for," Rowan surmised, her journalist's instinct evident.

Eclipse considered his response carefully. The energy field between them continued to resonate, creating harmonics that Eclipse found increasingly difficult to ignore. The wine from dinner had introduced variables into his system, subtle alterations in his normal control parameters.

"Partly," he said. "After sixty cycles of mediating essentially the same conflicts with diminishing results, I began to question the purpose."

"You lost faith in the possibility of resolution?" Rowan asked.

"I lost faith in the methodology," Eclipse clarified.

"Continued negotiation without substantive change is merely delay, not progress."

Rowan nodded, understanding. "So when this mission came up..."

"My coming on this mission wasn't my idea, but I did help plan it. This represented a different approach," Eclipse said. "And perhaps, though I did not acknowledge it at the time, an escape from the repetitive cycle."

"Only to find yourself still mediating between Solar and Lunar," Rowan noted with a small smile.

"An irony not lost on me," Eclipse agreed.

"What do you find the most confusing about Earth?" she asked, her tone low and soft.

"You." The answer was simple, honest.

"Me?" Rowan gave a small laugh of surprise.

"Yes." He nodded to emphasize his answer. "Your energy calls to me, yet you tell me to stop. Your body tells me to go to you. Your words say stop."

"Your skin-suit is deteriorating more rapidly," Rowan observed, reaching for his cheek. Her gentle touch stroked over the fake skin. "Around your eyes, especially."

Eclipse touched his face, feeling the thinning membrane. "The Earth atmosphere accelerates the breakdown of the polymers. The material was not designed for prolonged use."

"Does it hurt?" she asked.

"No. But it becomes increasingly restrictive as it degrades." He hesitated, then added, "In my natural state, my energy would flow more freely."

Rowan set down her tea and turned toward him more fully. "You can take it off, you know. I'm not afraid to see what you really look like."

Her breathing deepened, and he saw her heat signature calling to him.

The offer resonated with more meaning than the simple words could convey. Eclipse studied her expression, finding no fear or hesitation in her eyes, only genuine curiosity and something deeper, a desire for truth that reflected her fundamental nature.

"We were told our transitions can be intense for humans," he warned.

"I think we've established I'm not easily intimidated," Rowan replied with a small smile.

Eclipse set aside his mug and rose from the sofa, moving to stand away from the window where the neighbors could see him.

"I'll shut the blinds." She went to pull a string to hide the room from the outside.

With deliberate movements, he removed the outer Earth clothing. The skin-suit had a human phallus between the legs as a useless decoration that did not mimic his actual shape. Her attention focused on it as he reached for the release mechanism at the back of his neck.

The skin-suit peeled from his body with a soft hissing sound, and the constraining membrane fell away to reveal his true form. Unlike Solar's blazing golden light or Lunar's absorbing darkness, Eclipse's natural state was a balance of both.

Rowan's breath caught, and her eyes widened as she took in his true appearance. Eclipse remained perfectly still, allowing her to look at him. His body maintained a humanoid shape but was composed of twilight energy, a luminous purple-blue that shifted and flowed like the sky at dusk. Within this energy, patterns of light and shadow moved in complex interactions, never fully separating.

"You're beautiful," she said finally, approaching him slowly. "Like the evening sky given form."

"That is an accurate assessment," Eclipse acknowledged, his voice resonating more fully now that he wasn't constrained. He felt his body absorbing energy more easily from the atmosphere.

Rowan stopped just before him, her hand half-raised in an unspoken question. Eclipse inclined his head slightly, granting permission. Her fingers tentatively touched his chest, then with more confidence as she discovered that while his form appeared fluid, it maintained substance.

"It's like touching a warm current," she murmured, fascination evident in her voice. "I can feel the energy flowing, but it doesn't hurt. It tingles."

"Our compatibility allows for safe interaction," Eclipse explained. "Had our biorhythms been discordant, the contact might have been uncomfortable for you."

Rowan's hand moved from his chest to his face, tracing the contours that were now defined by energy rather than solid matter. Where she touched, the patterns within his form responded, swirling toward her fingers like liquid metal drawn to a magnet.

"When you touched me in my office and while I was driving," she said softly, "it felt like every nerve ending in my body was alive. Was that because of this? Your true form affecting me even through the skin-suit?"

"Yes," Eclipse confirmed. "As the membrane thinned, more of my actual energy was able to interact with yours. Our connection amplified the effect."

Her fingers continued their exploration, moving along his shoulder and down his arm. Each touch created new patterns in his energy field, ripples that Eclipse found increasingly difficult to moderate.

"And if we were to touch fully without any barriers between us," Rowan asked, her voice dropping lower, "what would that feel like?"

Eclipse studied her face, noting the dilation of her pupils, the flush spreading across her skin, and the quickening of her pulse visible at her throat. He saw heat rising from her. All were indicators of human arousal, but more significantly, her energy field pulsed in a way that harmonized perfectly with his own.

He wished humans had the words to describe his feelings so he could adequately describe them to her.

"It would be intense," he answered. "More so than before. Our energy fields would interact directly, creating resonance patterns that both physical forms would experience as pleasure."

"I love the literal way you talk," she said.

"I know no other way."

"Show me these—*how did you say it?*—resonance pleasure patterns," Rowan requested, her gaze steady despite the vulnerability of the request.

Eclipse raised his hand to her face, mirroring

her earlier touch but now with no barrier between his energy and her skin. The contact created an immediate surge, his twilight energy flowing like water over her flesh, seeking pathways of connection.

Rowan gasped, her eyes widening at the sensation.

"Oh," she breathed, leaning into his touch. "That's..."

"Too much?" Eclipse asked, prepared to withdraw.

"No," she said quickly, her hand covering his to keep it in place. "It's incredible. Like every cell in my body just woke up. My heart is beating so fast."

Encouraged by her response, Eclipse let his other hand rise to her waist, drawing her closer. Where they connected, his energy adapted to her form, creating a seamless interface between twilight essence and human biology. He could feel her heartbeat, the rush of blood through her veins, the electrical impulses of her nervous system, all harmonizing with his own energy patterns.

When their lips met, the resonance intensified exponentially. Eclipse felt Rowan's consciousness merge with his own, their perceptions overlapping in ways that transcended normal physical contact. He experienced her wonder, her desire, her curiosity. It all flowed through the connection.

"I can feel what you feel," she whispered against his mouth. "It's like being inside twilight."

"The resonance creates a feedback loop," Eclipse explained, his voice vibrating with the effort of maintaining control. "Our energies recognize compatible patterns and seek to harmonize."

Rowan's hands moved across his shoulders and chest, each touch creating new waves of resonance that rippled through his form. The sensations were unlike anything Eclipse had experienced on Zorveya, where energy interactions were carefully regulated and moderated.

"Your clothing," he said, his voice deepening as the resonance grew stronger. "It creates interference in the energy flow."

Understanding immediately, Rowan stepped back just enough to remove her dress, then her undergarments, until she stood before him as unadorned as he was. The ambient light gilded her skin with a soft glow, highlighting the curves and planes of her human form.

"Better?" she asked, a hint of vulnerability in her voice despite her boldness.

"Perfect," Eclipse answered truthfully. The

human form was comparable to his kind, but there were subtle differences. She had two soft pleasure portals that sat high on the chest. And her skin remained the same shade, more or less.

When they came together again, the reverberation was unimpeded by artificial barriers. Eclipse's energy field expanded to encompass her, creating a twilight cocoon around them both. Within this shared space, sensation amplified, every touch creating ripples that affected them equally.

They moved to the soft surface of the rug before the fireplace, sinking down together in a tangle of limbs and energy. Eclipse found himself fascinated by the duality of the experience. The solidity of Rowan's physical form contrasted with the fluid interaction of their energy fields. He explored her body with meticulous attention, learning which touches created the strongest resonance, which patterns of energy flow produced the most pleasure.

Rowan proved an equally dedicated student, quickly discovering that certain configurations of her fingers through his energy field created intense feedback loops that made his twilight essence pulse and flare. She giggled when she found a particularly sensitive nexus point at the base of his spine, where a specific touch caused his entire form to momentarily flare brighter.

"You're learning quickly," Eclipse observed, his voice vibrating with pleasure.

"I'm motivated," Rowan replied with a smile that was both playful and predatory.

As their exploration continued, the connection between them built toward a critical threshold. Eclipse felt the harmonics shifting into higher frequencies, creating overtones that vibrated through both his energy field and Rowan's physical form. She sensed it too, her movements becoming more urgent, her breathing quickening as the pleasure intensified.

Eclipse let his energy flow into every opening in her body, noting the damp place between her thighs was particularly reactive. When they finally joined completely, merging into a single harmonious whole, the resonance peaked. Eclipse's twilight essence flowed through Rowan's body like a tide, illuminating her from within as her own energy patterns rose to meet his. The boundaries between them blurred, creating a singular experience of shared sensation.

Rowan cried out as the first wave of completion washed over her, her body arching against his as pleasure surged through their connected fields. Eclipse felt her climax as if it were his own, the sensation amplified by the feedback loop between them. His own release followed moments later, twilight energy pulsing in waves that matched the rhythm of her body.

For several heartbeats, they existed in perfect harmony, two beings temporarily unified. Then slowly, gently, the fields began to disentangle, returning to their separate but connected states.

Rowan lay beneath him, breathless and wide-eyed, her skin glowing faintly with residual twilight energy.

"That was..." she began, then laughed softly. "I don't even have words."

"Words are often inadequate for energy experiences," Eclipse agreed, his form still flowing around and through her in gentle aftershocks.

"Is it always like that for your kind?" she asked, her fingers tracing patterns in his twilight essence.

"No," Eclipse admitted. "The resonance between us is unusually harmonic. It creates possibilities beyond typical interactions."

Rowan smiled at that, a slow, satisfied expression. "So I'm special?"

"You are unique in my experience," Eclipse

confirmed, his energy patterns shifting to reflect the truth of his statement.

They remained entwined, safe from the galaxy of problems outside.

"We should probably discuss Milano," Rowan said eventually, though she made no move to separate from him.

Well, almost safe.

"Tomorrow," Eclipse decided, surprising himself with the uncharacteristic postponement. "Some matters warrant immediate attention. Others benefit from careful consideration after proper rest."

Rowan laughed softly. "That sounds suspiciously like procrastination coming from a diplomat."

"Strategic delay," Eclipse corrected, his energy patterns reflecting amusement. "A recognized diplomatic technique."

She nestled closer, her body fitting perfectly against his form. Through their continued connection, Eclipse sensed her fatigue, the natural human need for sleep beginning to assert itself despite her desire to remain awake.

"Rest," he encouraged. "I will maintain vigilance."

"Stay with me?" she asked, her voice softening. "You won't disappear?"

"I will remain," Eclipse promised, his energy field adjusting to provide both warmth and comfort.

As Rowan's consciousness faded into dreams, Eclipse maintained their connection, feeling the shift in her energy patterns as her mind entered different states of activity. It was fascinating, this human cycle of wakefulness and sleep, so different from the constant awareness of Twilight existence.

Eclipse watched the progression of shadows along the edges of the closed blinds, marking the passage of Earth's night. His thoughts turned to the complications that would need to be addressed when morning came. Milano's interest in their arrival created new variables in an already complex equation. Solar and Lunar would need to be informed, and greater precautions taken.

Yet as he held Rowan against him, her breathing deep and regular in sleep, Eclipse found himself unwilling to focus solely on threats and contingencies. The connection between them had created something unexpected, a joining that transcended mere diplomatic objectives or biological compatibility.

For the first time since leaving for Earth, Eclipse felt a purpose beyond the mission parameters. He had a reason to remain that had nothing to do with proving coexistence was possible between opposing factions. Rowan had awakened something within him that decades of diplomatic service had slowly eroded. Genuine connection.

As the night deepened around them, Eclipse made a decision. Whatever came next, whatever threats Milano posed, whatever complications arose from their unplanned arrival, he would protect this connection. Not because the mission required it, but because it had become essential to his own existence.

Outside, a meteor streaked across the sky, a brief flare of light against the darkness. Eclipse watched its passage, thinking of journeys begun by chance and destinations discovered by necessity. Perhaps being exiled to Earth wasn't the chastisement the council had intended. Perhaps, in their attempt to remove him from the equation, they had inadvertently guided him toward something far more valuable than political influence.

Balance. Connection. Understanding. The core principles of the Twilight Belt given new meaning through one human woman who saw beyond appearances to the essence beneath.

Eclipse settled into watchful stillness, his energy field maintaining its protective cocoon around Rowan's sleeping form. Tomorrow would bring new challenges, but for now, in this moment of perfect harmony, he had found his own twilight zone, a place of balance between worlds.

And for the first time in many cycles, Eclipse felt truly at peace.

9

Rowan woke to the sensation of soft, humming energy caressing her skin. For a moment, she kept her eyes closed, savoring the impossible feeling of being wrapped in twilight. Her body felt different, like her nerves had been rewired overnight, each one now hyper-aware and tingling with lingering pleasure.

She'd had sex with an alien. An actual, honest-to-gods alien. And it had been transcendent.

She opened her eyes to find Eclipse watching her, his true form still unmasked, twilight energy flowing in mesmerizing patterns. In the morning light filtering through the blinds, he looked even more ethereal than he had last night, less solid, more like the embodiment of dusk itself.

"Good morning," she murmured, her voice husky from sleep.

"Your Earth greeting is accurate. The morning appears to possess positive attributes," Eclipse replied, his melodic voice vibrating through her more than just her ears.

Rowan couldn't help but smile. Even after the intimacy they'd shared, he still spoke like a scientific observer of human customs. It was oddly endearing.

"Did you sleep at all?" she asked, stretching languidly.

"My kind does not require unconsciousness for rejuvenation," Eclipse explained. "I maintained awareness while you cycled through your sleep patterns. Your delta waves were particularly harmonious."

"You watched my brainwaves while I slept?" Rowan propped herself up on one elbow. "That should probably creep me out, but somehow it doesn't."

"The resonance between us creates unusual acceptance parameters," Eclipse said, his energy field shifting closer to her. "Your tolerance for my alien characteristics defies predicted human responses."

"Yeah, well..." Rowan reached out to touch a swirling pattern in his twilight form. "After last night,

I'm pretty sure we're past the point of being weirded out by our differences."

The memory of their connection sent a flush of heat through her. She'd never experienced anything remotely like the way his energy had flowed through her, illuminating her from within, creating sensations that shouldn't have been physically possible.

Eclipse's form brightened in response to her touch. "The harmony between our energy patterns remains strong even after rest. This is uncommon."

"Uncommon good or uncommon bad?" Rowan asked, suddenly aware of the larger implications. She'd known him for all of two days. Two incredible, mind-blowing, reality-shattering days, but still. This was fast, even by alien abduction standards.

"Uncommon in its intensity and persistence," Eclipse clarified. "Such resonance typically requires extensive exposure and intentional attunement."

"So what you're saying is..." Rowan traced her fingers through his twilight essence, "we've got chemistry."

Eclipse seemed to consider this human term. "An oversimplification, but not inaccurate. Though quantum harmonic convergence would be more precise."

Rowan laughed, the sound bright in the quiet

morning. "Only you could make the fact that we're compatible sound like advanced physics."

The moment of levity faded as reality began creeping back in. Rowan glanced at her phone on the bedside table, checking the time.

"Shit. It's almost nine. I should have been at work an hour ago." She sat up, running her hands through her tangled hair. "And we still need to warn Solar and Lunar about Milano."

At the mention of Milano, Eclipse's form shifted, condensing slightly as if preparing for a defensive posture. "Yes. The corporation's interest in our arrival presents significant complications."

Rowan swung her legs over the edge of the bed, reluctantly leaving the warmth of Eclipse's nearness. "Understatement of the century. Milano doesn't just take an interest in things. They acquire them, study them, and usually weaponize whatever they learn. You need to be careful."

He nodded. "I will listen to your advice."

She stood and headed for the bathroom, talking over her shoulder. "I need to shower. Then we should head to the retreat. I'll call in and say I'm running late."

In the shower, the hot water cascading over her skin felt oddly flat compared to Eclipse's energy touch. Rowan tried to focus on the practical concerns ahead, but her mind kept circling back to the night before. She'd experienced something profound, something that had changed her. But they were also facing a very real threat.

Milano wouldn't stop with just observation. If they'd identified Eclipse and his companions as extraterrestrials, they would be marshaling resources for capture right now. James Petersen's appearance at dinner wasn't a coincidence. It was reconnaissance.

By the time Rowan emerged from the bathroom wrapped in a towel, Eclipse had resumed his humanoid form, the skin-suit reapplied though visibly deteriorating around his eyes and hands.

"Your suit is failing," she said more to herself as she headed to her closet.

"As I said before, the polymer matrix breaks down in Earth's atmosphere," Eclipse confirmed. "It was designed for short-term use only."

"Well, we'll need to figure something out." Rowan pulled clothes from her closet, deciding to wear practical jeans and a lightweight long-sleeve shirt. "If Milano's tracking you, we need to make you look as human as possible."

As she dressed, Rowan's journalist instincts

kicked into high gear, analyzing the situation from multiple angles.

"We need to know exactly what Milano knows and what they're looking for," she said, tugging on her boots. "And I need to understand what kind of danger you're in if they find you."

Eclipse moved to the window, carefully peering through the blinds at the street outside. "The danger extends to you as well, Rowan. Your association with us places you within their acquisition parameters."

A chill ran down Rowan's spine despite her attempt to stay practical. "Yeah, well, they were already on my shit list before you guys arrived."

She finished dressing and checked her phone again. Three missed calls from the retreat. She quickly dialed back.

"Duskrock Yoga and Spa, this is Darren," answered the retreat manager.

"Darren, it's Rowan. Sorry, I'm running late. Had a situation come up with those special guests in the Desert Suite. I'm heading in now."

"Actually," Darren sounded relieved, "I was calling to tell you that your schedule lightened. We've had a group cancellation due to the *incident*. Some corporate retreat from Phoenix. Apparently, their legal department advised against bringing executives to a location with unidentified aerial phenomena." He laughed nervously. "So we're pretty quiet. The VIPs in the Desert Suite still need attention, though. Stephanie said you booked it and they're to be left alone?"

"Yeah, I got them handled. Wannabe celebs needing complete privacy. You know those influencer types. Want to feel special, but they paid top dollar," Rowan lied. Her internal alarm bells went off. "What corporate retreat canceled?"

"Um, let me check... Milano Enterprises. They were booked under the name M.E. Tech. Ring any bells? They're pretty big in biotech, I think."

Rowan's blood ran cold. "Yeah, I've heard of them."

"Oh, hey, isn't that the company whose founder disappeared off the map a few years back? Yeah, yeah, he's that crazy billionaire who tried to build a rocket. There were those rumors that he was abducted by aliens, but others think he's living in a compound in South America or something."

"Oh, yeah, I remember seeing something about that on TV," Rowan dismissed. "Listen, Darren, I'll head straight to the Desert Suite and make sure our special guests are taken care of. I'll have my cell today if anything comes up. Thanks for letting me know."

She hung up, turning to Eclipse with wide eyes. "My manager said Milano had a corporate retreat booked. They canceled this morning."

Eclipse's expression remained calm, but his energy field visibly contracted. "Your manager has inadvertently provided valuable intelligence."

ECLIPSE RETRIEVED HIS EARTH CLOTHING.

"If they needed the retreat as a cover for surveillance operations, why cancel?" Rowan wondered, before answering for herself, "Because they saw us together last night and recognized me. They know I have full access to the retreat, including the security cameras. I could have kept an eye on them."

"We must relocate to the retreat immediately," Eclipse said. "Solar and Lunar need to be warned."

"If they don't already know." Rowan checked the windows and doors, making sure everything was locked before they left. Not that locks would stop Milano if they decided to search her place.

As they headed for her car, Rowan scanned the street with new wariness. The isolated neighborhood suddenly seemed full of potential threats. Why was that van parked down the street? Mrs. Lowen stared intently at it through her curtains.

In the car, Eclipse remained unnaturally still, his attention fixed on their surroundings. Rowan pulled out of her driveway, obsessively checking her rearview mirror.

"So what's the plan?" she asked, taking a route that would avoid the main roads. "If Milano's actively hunting you guys, we need a strategy."

"Strategy requires accurate intelligence," Eclipse replied. "We must first gather information about Milano's capabilities and objectives. Then we can formulate an appropriate response."

"Well, I can tell you their objective," Rowan said, her knuckles white on the steering wheel. "They want alien tech. Before I got shut down, I was investigating rumors that Milano had acquired unusual materials from a meteor crash site in New Mexico. They hushed it up, but my source claimed they extracted something with non-terrestrial properties."

Eclipse absorbed the information with a disturbing calm. "This suggests prior experience with extraterrestrial entities or artifacts. Their pursuit of us is likely informed by that knowledge."

"Which means they probably have specialized

equipment for tracking you," Rowan concluded. "God, this is insane. Two days ago my biggest problem was explaining to Mrs. Henderson why her chakra cleansing got rescheduled."

A flicker of something that might have been amusement passed through Eclipse's eyes. "Your adaptation to extraordinary circumstances continues to be remarkable."

"Trust me, I'm freaking out on the inside," Rowan admitted. She took a sharp turn onto a service road that wound behind the retreat. "I just happen to be good at compartmentalizing. A useful skill for both journalists and people whose alien boyfriends are being hunted by evil corporations."

The word boyfriend slipped out before Rowan could catch it. She winced internally. Way to put a label on something completely beyond human relationship categories.

"By boyfriend, I just mean you're a boy, kinda, and a friend, and—

"Your designation is not inaccurate, though limited by human relationship parameters. Our connection transcends typical biological pairing." Eclipse didn't seem bothered by the term.

"Right," Rowan muttered. "Not boyfriends. Just quantumly harmonically converged or whatever."

She pulled into the retreat's back entrance, parking in the staff area where her car wouldn't be easily visible from the main road. The morning was quiet, with few guests visible.

"The Desert Suite has a private entrance," Rowan explained as they exited the car. "We can go in without being seen from the main building."

They moved quickly across the grounds, staying close to the landscaping that provided cover. Rowan led Eclipse down a winding path to a secluded building set against the red rocks. The Desert Suite was the retreat's most exclusive accommodation, designed to blend with the natural landscape while providing luxury and privacy.

Rowan used her master key card to access the suite. Inside, the space was dim and quiet.

"Solar?" Eclipse called softly. "Lunar?"

No response.

"They must not have arrived yet," Rowan said, moving through the suite to check the rooms. Solar was supposed to be at The Crash Zone with Dani the night before, and Lunar was with Poppy. She hid a bemused smile. Maybe all of the aliens got lucky last night.

The suite was empty, but showed signs of recent occupation. The blackout curtains were up in the western room, and the full-spectrum lights she'd provided had been installed in the eastern one.

"I should try calling them," Rowan suggested, pulling out her phone.

Before she could dial, the door opened. Rowan spun around, heart pounding, only to see Stephanie saunter in.

"There you are!" Stephanie exclaimed. "I've been looking everywhere for you. Did you hear Milano canceled? Rumor is they're sending some bigwigs to investigate the UFO incident instead of running their stupid team building exercises." She paused, noticing Eclipse. "Oh, hello tall, dark, and literally stellar. Those contacts are amazing. Where did you get them?"

Eclipse glanced at Rowan, clearly unsure how to respond to Stephanie's rapid-fire speech.

"Steph, what are you doing in here?" Rowan asked, moving to block Eclipse from view. She cared about Stephanie, but also accepted that her friend couldn't be trusted with a secret this big.

"Introduce me," Stephanie whispered, trying to push past. "What is your name, handsome?"

"My name is Eclipse." He took Rowan's phone from her and moved away from them. She watched him lift it to his ear and wondered if he faked a phone call to avoid Stephanie.

It didn't work.

"Eclipse? Cool name." Stephanie tried to move further into the suite, oblivious to the tension. "So, are you guys hiding out here or what? And have you seen that hottie with the gold highlights? He was at The Crash Zone last night with the fire dancer. The whole place went nuts when the lights started flickering."

Eclipse maintained his diplomat's composure and dropped his arm. "Solar is expected to arrive shortly."

"Solar? Another space name? What are you guys, some kind of astronomy club?" Stephanie laughed, turning to go to one of the sofas as if to make herself at home.

Rowan grabbed her friend's arm and pulled her toward the door. "You can't just walk in here."

"Ow, hey," Stephanie protested, trying to pull away.

"Steph, I'm serious," Rowan persisted, forcing her from the room. When they were alone outside, she said, "Are you trying to get me fired? They paid for complete privacy. Not even housekeepers. You can't just walk into the guest suites unannounced.

With all of the cancellations, we need to keep these guests happy."

"Whatever. Fine, keep the hottie rich guys all to yourself." Stephanie looked a little hurt. "I'm just glad you're not hanging out with corporate drones like the Milano people. They gave me the creeps when they checked in yesterday."

Rowan frowned. "Milano checked in? I thought they canceled. When?"

"The team building conference room package thing was canceled. I told you, the bigwigs came instead yesterday afternoon. They're all suits and serious faces." Stephanie shuddered dramatically. "They kept asking questions about the UFO sighting and whether any unusual individuals had been seen around the retreat afterward."

A cold knot formed in Rowan's stomach. "What did you tell them?"

Stephanie rolled her eyes. "Please. Don't look so worried. Like I'd tell those Men-in-Black asshats anything. I said we get all kinds of weirdos in Duskrock, especially after UFO reports. They'd have to be more specific." She grinned. "Though I did mention my video went viral, just to mess with them."

"You what?" Rowan's voice rose sharply.

"Relax," Stephanie waved dismissively. "They seemed super interested in seeing it. I told them to follow my page. I swear I didn't say anything to make them cancel the corporate retreat. Darren said that was their lawyers."

"Where are they now?"

"I don't know. Some of them checked out this morning. But one of them—*James something*—left his card at the front desk for you." Stephanie dug in her pocket. She handed over James Petersen's business card. It was the same one he'd left on their table the night before.

"Thanks," Rowan said, taking the card. "That's helpful."

"I know, right? I'm not just a pretty face." Stephanie started backing away toward the main building. "Anyway, I should get back to the front desk before Darren notices I'm gone. Text me if the hot sparkly guy comes back. Or his dark broody friend. They're both totally my type. Those two can beam me up to their spaceship anytime, if you know what I mean."

"You're oversexed," Rowan teased.

"Don't slut shame," Stephanie scolded with a laugh.

Rowan watched Stephanie leave before

returning to the suite. She collapsed onto the sofa, suddenly exhausted. "Milano's been at the retreat since yesterday. They're already talking to the staff."

"They move with considerable efficiency," Eclipse noted, his tone neutral but his body seemed to pulse with concern.

"We need to warn Solar and Lunar to be careful coming back before they walk into a trap," Rowan said, taking her phone from Eclipse. She had hired the woman to perform for the retreat and found her likable.

"Solar is aware of the danger," Eclipse stated, pointing at the hotel phone "He called that device when you were scolding the woman."

"I wasn't scolding her."

"You spoke to her for a long time, and I felt the annoyance in your energy patterns even through the door," he countered.

Rowan gave a small laugh. "Maybe I was scolding her a little. She's harmless, but she has boundary issues. And she's a complete gossip. The woman never met a story she didn't want to spread around the internet."

"We do not wish to be a story on your overlord devices," he stated.

"Noted. I'll text Poppy again and try to see where

she and Lunar are at." As she typed, the door opened. Rowan jumped, but it was Solar who entered, wearing a hoodie topped by a cowboy hat, and sunglasses that barely contained his golden glow.

Dani followed close behind him. Her expression was tense.

"Eclipse," Solar acknowledged.

"Solar," Eclipse greeted with obvious relief. "Your disguise is effective."

Rowan disagreed with that assessment, but kept quiet. Solar

"Yes. It is," Solar replied, moving past him into the suite. "I am a cowboy."

Dani met Rowan's eyes and gave a small shrug. "He found the hat in my car."

Rowan stood. "I'm glad you're all right."

Solar gave a small frown at her concern, as if he didn't know how to respond to it.

"We need to discuss Milano and the extraction timeline," Solar said, removing the glasses now that they were in secure quarters. "Where is Lunar?"

"Unknown," Eclipse admitted. "He also did not return last night."

"Hopefully still with Poppy," Rowan suggested, trying not to think about what would happen if Milano had found him first. "I just texted her again to let her know Milano is at the retreat. I told them to be careful."

Solar continued to frown. "We must locate him immediately. Milano is actively tracking us, and Galaxy Brides has set extraction for forty-eight hours from now."

Rowan felt her heart skip.

"They contacted you?" she whispered, trying to keep her voice steady despite the sudden flood of emotion.

Extraction. They were leaving in forty-eight hours. Eclipse was leaving. After everything they'd shared, after the connection they'd formed, he would be gone in two days.

She pushed the thought aside, focusing on the immediate threat.

"A Milano representative approached us at dinner last night," Eclipse said. "James Petersen. He mentioned unusual atmospheric disturbances and electromagnetic anomalies."

"They're using satellite technology and ground teams with specialized equipment," Solar added.

"That tracks with what I uncovered before they shut down my investigation," Rowan nodded, her journalist's mind connecting the dots despite her emotional turmoil. "The Milano Foundation has been funding unusual research for years, supposedly for medical applications, but the security around their facilities was military-grade."

"So what's the plan?" Dani asked, looking between them. "Are you guys leaving?"

The question hung in the air, heavy with implications. Rowan stared at Eclipse, eager and scared to hear his answer.

"That decision has not been finalized." Eclipse didn't meet her gaze. "We must discuss all options once Lunar is located."

Rowan took a deep breath and pretended to check the cupboards in the kitchenette. Her hands shook. She needed to get control of her emotions.

"I can call Poppy," Dani said behind her. "They're probably at her place. It's out near Boynton Canyon."

As Dani made the call, Eclipse joined Solar on the far side of the room by the window. Rowan tried to hear what they were saying, but it was too soft.

After a long moment, Dani's voice interrupted their conversation. "Good news and bad news. I reached Poppy, and Lunar is with her. That's the good news."

"And the bad?" Rowan asked.

"They spotted men in black SUVs near her place this morning. Professional types with equipment.

They're hiding out in some cave system Poppy knows."

Solar and Eclipse exchanged glances.

"Milano has begun active pursuit," Solar stated.

"Poppy says she can bring Lunar here tonight after dark," Dani continued. "But they're staying put until then. Something about him being more mobile at night?"

"His shadow-walking abilities are enhanced in darkness," Eclipse explained. "A wise precaution."

"So what do we do until then?" Dani asked.

"We prepare defenses, gather intelligence on Milano's activities, and develop contingency plans for multiple scenarios," Solar said.

"I can help with the intelligence part," Rowan offered, trying to meet Eclipse's gaze. There was so much she suddenly wanted to say to him, but couldn't. It wasn't the right time. "I still have contacts who might know what Milano is up to locally."

Solar nodded, as if appreciating her tactical thinking.

"We should also prepare for the possibility that Galaxy Brides' extraction may be compromised," he added. "If Milano has tracking capability for alien technology, they may detect any attempt to remove us from Earth."

"So we're talking about a potential showdown," Dani summarized. "Aliens versus shadowy government contractors."

"A scenario I had hoped to avoid," Eclipse admitted. "Our mission was supposed to be a peaceful cultural exchange."

"Sometimes peace isn't an option," Solar replied. "Sometimes you must fight to protect what matters."

Rowan didn't speak as she studied the others. This was bigger than just a few lost aliens. This was about stopping a corporation with near-unlimited resources from getting its hands on advanced alien technology.

Plus, she had to admit, she'd enjoy the chance to take them down after what they did to her.

"Okay," she said, taking charge. "We need a plan. First, we need to secure this location. Second, we need intel on Milano's movements. Third, we need to coordinate with Lunar and Poppy to ensure their safe arrival."

Eclipse finally met her eyes, and Rowan felt that familiar pulse of energy between them.

"I've covered war zones," she explained with a shrug. "Different kind of conflict, same basic principles."

Dani had moved to the window, peering out

through the blinds. "Do you think they'd try something here? At the retreat with all these witnesses?"

"If they're as desperate as they seem, witnesses won't matter," Rowan said grimly. "They'd just spin it as arresting dangerous individuals. They've got PR people who can make kidnapping sound like public service."

Solar's golden form brightened with what Rowan had come to recognize as agitation. "I require direct combat data. What weapons do these Milano operatives typically employ?"

"Based on what I uncovered before they shut me down, they have access to military-grade hardware. Think tranquilizer darts, stun weapons, maybe even specialized containment equipment if they've dealt with non-humans before." Rowan turned to Eclipse. "Your energy form, can it be contained by physical barriers?"

"Certain energy-dampening fields would be effective," Eclipse confirmed. "Though Earth technology should not be capable of generating such fields."

"Unless they reverse-engineered something from previous alien encounters," Rowan pointed out. "Or even scavenged equipment. I think we have to assume they have tools we don't know about."

The realization hung heavy in the air. There was no telling what capabilities they might have developed.

"I agree. We should assume the worst," Dani said, crossing her arms. "That they can track you, catch you, and contain you."

"Then we must ensure they do not have the opportunity," Solar declared. "I will scout the perimeter of this facility."

"No," Eclipse and Rowan said simultaneously.

Rowan continued, "You're the most visible of the three. Your energy creates electrical disturbances. If they have any kind of detection equipment, you'll set it off like a Christmas tree."

"Christmas tree?" Solar frowned in confusion.

"Bright lights, very noticeable," Dani explained. "She's right. You'd be spotted immediately."

Eclipse nodded. "I should conduct reconnaissance instead. My twilight energy signature is more adaptable, less detectable in transitional light conditions."

Rowan felt a stab of fear at the thought of Eclipse out there, potentially exposed to Milano's operatives. "Or we could use perfectly normal humans who won't register on alien detection equipment."

"That would place you in danger," Eclipse objected.

"Less danger than you'd be in," Rowan countered. "They're looking for aliens, not retreat staff. Dani and I can move around freely without raising suspicion."

Solar looked between them. "The logic is sound, though the risk remains substantial."

"I've handled risk before," Rowan said firmly. "And we need information more than we need to hide right now."

Eclipse moved closer to her, his energy field rippling with concern. "What do you propose?"

"Dani and I will do a casual walk around the grounds. Check out the parking areas, note any suspicious vehicles or people. Standard surveillance, nothing that would draw attention." Rowan met his gaze steadily. "Meanwhile, you two stay here, out of sight, and work on a plan for extraction. If Galaxy Brides is coming in forty-eight hours, we need to be ready."

The mention of extraction sent another pang through her chest. Forty-eight hours. It wasn't enough time. Not nearly enough to figure out what this thing between her and Eclipse was, or could be. Part of her wanted to stay behind and embrace every second she could with him.

"I'll go with Rowan," Dani agreed. "Two women walking around a retreat won't raise any red flags."

Solar looked displeased but nodded. "You will report any signs of surveillance or potential threat immediately."

"Of course," Dani agreed. "And if we don't come back in an hour, assume we've been captured and mount a daring rescue." She grinned, though the tension in her shoulders betrayed her attempt at levity.

Rowan flinched. These guys tended to take things literally. Very literally.

"That will not be necessary," Eclipse stated with unexpected firmness. "We will maintain contact. If communication is lost, we will locate you immediately."

Rowan believed he would without question. The intensity of his gaze reinforced that he wasn't making an idle promise.

"Alright," Rowan said, checking her phone. "We'll head out, do a quick circuit of the grounds, and be back within the hour. If we see anything suspicious, we'll text Dani's phone immediately."

Dani handed her phone to Solar.

As they prepared to leave, Eclipse drew Rowan

slightly aside. "Your willingness to accept risk on our behalf is significant."

Rowan looked up at him, searching those star-filled eyes. "I'm not just doing this for you. Milano tried to destroy my career and my life once. I'm not letting them get away with it again."

"Even so," Eclipse said softly, "be cautious. The connection between us... It would be regrettable if it were severed prematurely."

Coming from anyone else, it might have sounded cold. From Eclipse, it was practically a declaration of love. Rowan felt her heart lurch.

"I'll be careful," she promised. "Just don't make any decisions about that extraction until we've had a chance to talk. Okay?"

Eclipse tilted his head slightly. "I will defer such decisions until we have discussed all variables."

It wasn't exactly the passionate response she might have hoped for, but from a twilight diplomat, it was something. Rowan nodded and turned to join Dani at the door.

"Ready?" Dani asked.

"As I'll ever be," Rowan replied. She cast one last look at Eclipse before they slipped out into the morning sunlight, leaving the aliens in the suite.

10

THE SUN BEAT DOWN ON ROWAN'S NECK AS SHE and Dani stepped out of the Desert Suite. What had seemed like a peaceful retreat just days ago now felt like a minefield, every shadow potentially concealing Milano operatives.

"Act normal," Rowan murmured, plastering on her best customer service smile as they passed a group of tourists taking selfies by the meditation garden.

They rounded the corner toward the main building when Rowan spotted a man in an unmarked black polo, his hand pressed to an earpiece, eyes scanning methodically across the grounds. His gaze locked with Rowan's for a fraction of a second before she deliberately looked away, pointing at a nearby cactus as if showing Dani an interesting feature.

"Don't look now, but security guy at two o'clock," she said through her fixed smile. Her journalistic instincts tingled and her heart beat faster. This reminded her of the time she was overseas covering a desert op. "Earpiece, tactical stance, trying too hard to blend in."

"Got it," Dani replied, pretending to laugh at something Rowan said. "So what's our actual plan here? Just stroll around and hope they don't grab us?"

"Basically," Rowan admitted. "But we need to—"

A sharp electronic whine cut through the air overhead. Rowan's heart leapt into her throat as she instinctively looked up.

A black drone hovered thirty feet above them, its camera lens adjusting with mechanical precision. Focused directly on them.

"Shit," Dani whispered. "I think our cover's blown. That didn't take long."

"Keep walking," Rowan instructed, fighting the urge to run. "If they wanted to grab us, they would have already."

The drone followed their movement, maintaining a consistent distance as they continued down the path. The hairs on Rowan's arms stood

up. This wasn't just surveillance. It was intim-
idation.

They approached the retreat's main pool area,
where a handful of guests lounged in the morning
sun. Rowan spotted two more men in tactical
clothing poorly disguised as maintenance workers,
their attention too focused, movements too
deliberate.

"They're herding us," Rowan realized, noticing
how the men had positioned themselves to block
certain exit paths.

"What?"

"They're channeling us away from the Desert
Suite." Rowan's mind raced. "They want to separate
us from Solar and Eclipse."

As if confirming her suspicion, her phone
buzzed. An unknown number had sent a text, *"Ms.
Clark. Please proceed to the front entrance. Mr.
Petersen would like a word."*

She showed Dani the screen.

"They're tracking your phone," Dani said, her
voice tight. "We need to ditch it."

"No," Rowan replied, an idea forming. "We need
to use it."

She quickly typed back, *"On my way. Give me
10 minutes to finish showing my guest around."*

"What are you doing?" Dani hissed.

"Buying time. And confirming who we're dealing with." Rowan slipped her phone back into her pocket. "Now we need to move. Fast."

They veered toward a small garden shed that housed pool equipment. Rowan used her master key to unlock it, pulling Dani inside and closing the door behind them. The space was cramped and smelled of chlorine.

"Okay, so we've established that Milano has the place surrounded," Dani whispered. "Can we go back now?"

"Not yet." Rowan peered through a small window. "We need to figure out how many operatives they have and what kind of equipment they're using." She counted three more men taking positions around the perimeter. "If we go straight back, they'll just follow us to Eclipse and Solar."

A metallic clank sounded on the shed's roof. Both women froze.

The drone had landed directly above them.

"I think they're scanning for us," Rowan whispered, remembering what Eclipse had said about energy signatures. "If they've developed technology to track the aliens..."

A sharp electronic beep confirmed her fears. The drone had detected something.

"We need to move. Now." Rowan grabbed a pool skimmer from the wall and shoved the door open. In one fluid motion, she swung the pole upward, catching the drone's propellers. The machine sputtered and careened sideways, crashing into a cactus.

"Run!" she shouted, abandoning all pretense of casual reconnaissance.

They sprinted across the pool deck, startling sunbathers as they dashed past. Behind them, shouts erupted as Milano operatives abandoned their cover. Rowan glanced back to see three men in pursuit, hands reaching inside jackets for what she feared were weapons.

"This way!" Dani veered sharply left, toward the retreat's open-air yoga pavilion.

A class was in session with twenty guests in various poses on their mats. Rowan and Dani slowed to a power walk, weaving between the participants.

"Sorry, maintenance emergency," Rowan apologized to the bewildered instructor as they passed through. The Milano men halted at the edge of the pavilion, unwilling to cause a scene with so many witnesses.

The women exited through the far side, immediately breaking into a run again. Rowan's lungs burned as they sprinted down a service path that cut between two guest buildings.

"We can't lead them back to the suite," Dani gasped.

"I know," Rowan panted. "We need to split up."

They reached a junction in the path. Ahead lay the main building, and, to the right, a narrow trail wound toward the red rocks at the property's edge.

"Take the trail," Rowan instructed. "Circle around the canyon side. I'll create a diversion."

"What? No!" Dani protested. "They're after you specifically."

"Exactly." Rowan was already backing toward the main building. "I'll be fine. Get to Eclipse and Solar. Tell them Milano is actively hunting us, not just watching. Don't contact my phone. Don't come after me."

Before Dani could argue further, Rowan turned and sprinted toward the retreat's central facility. Her phone buzzed again, *"Ms. Clark, your cooperation would make this much easier for everyone. We only want to talk."*

She didn't answer it, pushing through the staff entrance and weaving through the kitchen. The chef called out in surprise, but she didn't slow down. She hurried through the dining area, past startled guests, and into the lobby.

James Petersen stood by the reception desk, flanked by two security types. His expression shifted from confident to alarmed when he saw her burst in alone.

"Ms. Clark," he began.

Rowan didn't stop. She angled toward the gift shop, knocking over a display of crystal healing kits as she passed. The clatter and crash created momentary confusion.

"Security threat! Gun!" she shouted to the front desk attendant, pointing toward James. "Call the police!"

The lobby erupted into chaos as guests reacted to the commotion. Rowan used the distraction to slip into the manager's office, locking the door behind her. Darren wasn't in, thank god for small favors. She grabbed his desk phone and punched in a number from memory.

"Pete's Crystal Emporium and Alien First Contact Landmark," a voice answered over woodwind, ethereal music. "Your verified source for intergalactic connectedness and spiritual—"

"Pete, it's Rowan from Yoga and Spa. Remember

that alien flash mob contingency plan you've been going on about?"

"Hell yeah I do!"

"I'm calling in a code green. Now's your chance. Milano Enterprises is here hunting for aliens. Bring everyone. Costumes, props, the works. Make it big and loud."

"Are you serious? This isn't a prank?"

Someone pounded on the office door. "Ms. Clark! Open up!"

"Dead serious. Keep an eye out for Dani the fire dancer. We got separated. Get her to safety if you find her." Rowan replied. "And Pete? Make it fast. Code green. Code green. This is not a drill!"

She hung up as the pounding intensified. The window was her only option. She pried it open and squeezed through just as the door splintered inward.

Outside again, Rowan darted between buildings, keeping low. Milano operatives were everywhere now, their pretense at covert surveillance abandoned. She spotted two more black SUVs pulling into the retreat's entrance, disgorging additional personnel.

This was worse than she'd imagined. They weren't just investigating. This was a full-scale extraction operation.

Her phone buzzed yet again. This time, it wasn't

a text but a photo of a thermal image of what appeared to be the Desert Suite, with two distinct heat signatures visible inside. One blazing like a small sun, the other a strange, shifting pattern unlike anything human.

The message below it was simple, *"We already know what they are, Ms. Clark. And where. Cooperation now could save their lives."*

Cold fear sliced through Rowan. They were going to raid the suite. Eclipse and Solar were trapped.

She changed direction, abandoning stealth for speed. She had to warn them, had to reach them before Milano did. Her lungs burned as she sprinted along the perimeter path, taking the longest route to avoid Milano personnel.

The back service entrance to the Desert Suite came into view. No sign of operatives yet. They must have been mobilizing for a coordinated assault.

Rowan fumbled with her key card, hands shaking as she swiped it through the reader. The door unlocked with an agonizing delay, and she tumbled inside, slamming it shut behind her.

"They're coming!" she gasped. "Milano has thermal imaging of you both. They're preparing to raid the suite."

Eclipse and Solar turned from what appeared to be an impromptu defensive barricade of furniture. Solar's golden energy pulsed erratically, causing the lights to flicker and surge.

"Where is Dani?" Solar demanded.

"Circling around. She's safe." Rowan struggled to catch her breath. "But we won't be for long. They sent me this." She showed them the thermal image.

Eclipse studied it, his expression grave. "Their technology is more advanced than anticipated."

"We need to move," Rowan insisted. "Now. Before they surround us completely."

"The extraction coordinates are in the desert," Solar said. "We must reach them before extraction."

"And Lunar is still out there with Poppy," Eclipse added.

A heavy thud sounded at the front entrance. Then another.

Solar's form brightened dangerously. "Let them come. I will show them the power of Solarus."

"No!" Eclipse and Rowan exclaimed simultaneously.

"If you attack, they'll know exactly what they're dealing with," Rowan explained. "We need to escape, not engage."

Eclipse moved to the back window, peering out

cautiously. "The cliff face provides cover to the west. If we can reach the canyon trail—"

A deafening crash interrupted him as the front door burst from its hinges. Smoke billowed in, some kind of tactical grenade designed to disorient.

Solar reacted instinctively, his golden energy surging outward. The electronics in the room exploded in showers of sparks. The smoke dispersed in an unnatural ripple of superheated air.

Two figures in tactical gear appeared in the doorway, aiming what looked like specialized weapons. Not guns. Energy dampeners, if Rowan had to guess.

"Take cover!" Eclipse shouted, pushing Rowan behind the barricade.

One of the Milano operatives fired. A pulse of strange blue energy shot across the room, narrowly missing Solar and hitting the wall. Where it struck, the material seemed to warp and freeze simultaneously.

Solar roared in response, his human disguise burning away as his true form emerged, a being of pure golden light and fire. Heat rolled off him in waves that distorted the air itself.

"Stay down," Eclipse instructed Rowan, his own form shifting as the skin-suit dissolved completely.

His twilight energy expanded, creating a shield of dusk-like atmosphere around them both.

The second operative fired at Eclipse, but the energy pulse dissipated harmlessly into his twilight field.

"The rear exit," Eclipse urged. "When I create a diversion, run."

Before Rowan could protest, Eclipse's form expanded dramatically, filling the suite with twilight energy that obscured everything in a purple-blue haze. The operatives' shouted commands were muffled, distant. It became difficult to breathe in the new atmosphere.

"Now!" Eclipse's voice resonated from everywhere at once.

Rowan scrambled toward the back door, unable to see more than a few feet ahead through the twilight field. Behind her, she heard Solar unleash his power. It sounded like a solar flare erupting, followed by the operatives' screams.

Her hand found the door handle just as something massive crashed through the front of the suite. More Milano forces. More weapons. They were out of time.

Eclipse materialized beside her, his energy

contracting back into a roughly humanoid shape.
"Go!"

They burst through the rear exit together, Solar
following in a blaze of golden light that left scorch
marks on the door frame. Outside, the desert sun beat
down mercilessly, but there were no Milano operatives in sight. They'd committed their forces to the
frontal assault.

"This way," Rowan gasped, leading them toward
a narrow trail that snaked up the red rock formation
behind the suite.

As they climbed, shouts and alarms rose from
below. Rowan glanced back to see the Milano team
pouring out of the ruined suite, pointing up at them.
Several raised weapons.

"Faster," Eclipse urged, his twilight form flowing
over the rocks with unnatural grace.

Solar, by contrast, left smoldering footprints in
his wake, his golden energy barely contained as he
ascended.

They reached a ridge just as the first energy
pulse struck the rocks beside them, sending fragments flying. Rowan felt a sharp sting as a splinter of
stone cut her cheek.

"Keep moving," she panted, blood trickling down

her face. "There's a cave system up ahead. We can lose them there."

The trail narrowed dangerously, hugging the cliff face with a sheer drop to one side. Rowan's legs trembled with exertion and fear as she navigated the precarious path. Eclipse stayed close behind her, his energy occasionally brushing against her skin in what felt like reassurance.

Solar brought up the rear, periodically turning to send pulses of energy down the path, creating obstacles for their pursuers.

They rounded a bend, and the mouth of a cave appeared as a dark opening in the red rock face. Rowan stumbled toward it, legs burning from the climb.

"In here," she gasped, ducking into the darkness.

The temperature dropped immediately as they entered the cave system. Shafts of sunlight penetrated through cracks in the ceiling, providing just enough illumination to navigate.

"These caves connect throughout the canyon," Rowan explained, catching her breath. "The local indigenous peoples used them for centuries. Some parts are too narrow for adults to pass through, but there are routes to the other side."

Unfortunately, she didn't know those routes. It

would be just as easy to get lost forever underground. But that was a problem for later. Now they needed to escape danger.

Eclipse's twilight form provided a soft glow in the dimness. "Your knowledge of this terrain is invaluable."

The comment made her feel guilty.

"I've hiked here since I arrived in Duskrock," she replied. "Never thought I'd be using the caves to escape an alien manhunt."

Solar remained near the entrance, his golden light a beacon that would surely give away their position. "They are still pursuing," he reported. "Their thermal imaging technology will make concealment difficult."

Rowan's mind raced. "Deeper in, there's an underground stream. Maybe the water will mask thermal signatures?"

At least, she thought there was. She couldn't remember for sure if this was the cave she was thinking of.

They moved further into the cave system, the passageway narrowing until they had to proceed single file. Solar's energy illuminated strange petroglyphs on the walls, ancient drawings that depicted stars, spirals, and humanoid figures.

"Look," Rowan pointed with a tiny laugh. "The original UFO enthusiasts."

Eclipse examined the markings with interest. "Your species has long looked to the stars."

"And apparently met visitors before," Rowan added, indicating a petroglyph that showed tall beings descending from the sky.

A distant shout echoed through the cave. Milano forces had entered the system.

"Those do not represent any species I have met. We must keep moving," Solar urged.

The passage twisted and branched. Rowan led them down a narrower offshoot that required them to crouch. The sound of running water caused her to sigh in relief. They kept moving, and it grew louder. Soon they emerged into a larger chamber where an underground stream cut across their path.

"We need to wade upstream," Rowan said. "The water's only about knee-deep, but I'm warning you, it's freezing. It comes from deep underground."

She stepped into the stream, gasping as the cold water soaked through her jeans. Eclipse followed without hesitation, his twilight energy rippling oddly where it touched the water. Solar paused at the edge, his golden form hissing as steam rose where he contacted the stream.

"The water dampens my energy," he said, voice strained. "It will be difficult to maintain form."

"It's our best chance to mask our trail," Rowan insisted.

Reluctantly, Solar entered the stream. Steam filled the cave, making it instantly humid. His light noticeably dimmed, and he moved with obvious discomfort as they waded upstream.

The cold numbed Rowan's legs as she pushed forward. It became hard to walk. Behind them, shouts and the beams of flashlights indicated Milano was gaining ground.

"There should be a side passage ahead," Rowan said through chattering teeth. "It leads to a higher chamber that eventually exits on the canyon rim."

They reached the passage, pulling themselves out of the stream onto a rocky ledge. Solar immediately brightened, his energy regenerating now that he was free.

"The passage narrows ahead," Rowan warned, already crawling forward. "We have to go single file. Be careful."

Eclipse flowed into the tunnel behind her, his twilight form adapting to the confined space. The rocky surface scraped Rowan's palms and knees as she navigated the cramped passage. Water dripped from her soaked clothes, leaving a trail she hoped would blend into the landscape's natural discoloration.

"How much farther?" Solar called from behind, his voice strained. The passage was clearly compressing his energy.

"I don't know exactly," Rowan admitted. But where else could they go but forward? "These caves are extensive. But if we keep climbing, we should reach—"

A blue pulse of energy struck the rock wall inches from her head, sending stone fragments flying. Rowan flinched, covering her face.

"They've found us," Solar shouted.

Eclipse's energy surged protectively around Rowan. "Continue forward. I will delay them."

"No!" Rowan grabbed at his twilight form as it began to flow past her. "We stay together!"

Another energy pulse hit, closer this time. The narrow passage amplified the sound, making Rowan's ears ring.

"There's no time to argue," Eclipse insisted. "The passage is too confined for effective defense. You must reach the surface and contact the others."

Before she could protest further, Eclipse's form compressed impossibly thin, slipping past her and flowing back toward their pursuers like liquid shadow.

"Eclipse!" Rowan called after him.

Solar hooked her by the waist and easily pushed her in the other direction. "Move! His sacrifice will be meaningless if we are captured as well."

Sacrifice.

The word sent ice through Rowan's veins despite her rational mind telling her that Eclipse couldn't be killed by conventional weapons. She hoped that was true and highly doubted it was. She scrambled forward with renewed urgency, ignoring the scrapes on her hands as she clawed her way through the narrowing passage.

Behind them, flashes of purple-blue light illuminated the tunnel, accompanied by shouts and the distinctive sound of the energy weapons discharging. Eclipse was fighting, buying them time.

The passage suddenly opened into a larger chamber. Rowan tumbled out, Solar right behind her, his golden light revealing a cavernous space with multiple tunnels branching off in different directions.

"Which way?" Solar demanded, his form pulsing with agitation.

Rowan spun around, trying to orient herself. "I... I'm not sure." The admission felt like acid in her throat. She was completely lost. "I've never been this deep in the system."

A distant, muffled boom shook the cave, sending small rocks pattering from the ceiling. Solar's light flared in response. Rowan started to cry out and muffled her mouth with her hands. Tears streamed down her cheeks.

"Eclipse." Rowan felt a wave of panic rising. "We need to go back for him."

"He would want us to continue," Solar insisted. "To warn the others."

Another rumble, stronger this time, sent a shower of dust raining down on them. Cracks appeared in the chamber's ceiling. Each vibration felt like an accusation. They had abandoned Eclipse in the caves.

"The structure is destabilizing," Solar observed. "Eclipse's energy must be interacting with their weapons."

Rowan's mind raced, torn between going back for Eclipse and pressing forward to safety. A memory surfaced, something she'd read about local cave systems. The main passages followed underground water channels. If they kept following them, it would take them up or out.

They ducked into the tunnel just as another

explosion shook the caves. This passage was larger, allowing them to move more quickly. Time felt out of alignment in the cave. They rushed and hid, but constant fear made minutes seem like seconds. Solar's light illuminated their path, revealing more petroglyphs and strange mineral formations. At one point, they had to stop so he could find a sliver of sunlight to recharge.

"What exactly are these weapons Milano possesses?" Solar asked as they climbed higher through the winding passage. "They are not familiar to me."

"I don't know," Rowan admitted.

They emerged into another chamber where the ceiling rose high above them, disappearing into darkness. Shafts of sunlight penetrated through cracks in the rock, creating spotlights on the cave floor.

"We're getting closer to the surface," Rowan said, hope kindling in her chest.

A flash of movement in the shadows made her freeze. Solar immediately dimmed his light, but it was too late.

"Don't move," a voice ordered.

They'd been found.

11

Eclipse flowed backward through the narrow tunnel, his twilight essence compressing into the confined space as he moved away from Rowan and Solar. Every instinct urged him to stay with her, to protect her directly, but logic dictated otherwise. If Milano captured all of them, there would be no hope.

One of them had to create a diversion.

The energy weapons Milano wielded were unlike anything Eclipse expected to encounter on Earth. They were clearly derived from non-terrestrial technology. The blue pulses disturbed his twilight field in ways that suggested precise calibration for energy-based lifeforms.

They knew exactly what they were hunting.

Eclipse reached the wider section of the tunnel

where the underground stream cut across the path. Shouts and flashlight beams reflected off the water. Milano operatives waded upstream, all six of them equipped with the specialized weapons and what appeared to be scanning devices.

Eclipse expanded his twilight form to fill the chamber, becoming a diffuse purple-blue mist that clung to the ceiling and walls. The first operative emerged into the chamber, his scanner emitting an urgent beeping as it detected Eclipse's energy signature.

"Contact!" the man shouted, raising his weapon toward the ceiling.

Eclipse surged forward, enveloping the operative in twilight energy. The man fired wildly, the blue pulse dissipating harmlessly into Eclipse's diffuse form. Eclipse concentrated his energy around the man's weapon, disrupting its power source. The device overloaded with a crackle of electricity, forcing the operative to drop it with a yelp of pain.

"Williams is down! Target is—" Another operative's shout cut off as Eclipse swept through the chamber, creating a disorienting whirlwind of twilight energy. The man grabbed his head, screaming in pain.

Eclipse had never used his abilities as weapons

before. On Zorveya, he was a diplomat, a mediator, the twilight between extremes. But here, with Rowan's safety at stake, he found himself drawing on aspects of his nature he'd rarely explored.

The Milano team regrouped, forming a defensive circle. Their leader barked commands into a communication device, *"Target Twilight is engaged. Proceed with containment protocol Echo."*

Two operatives fired simultaneously, their energy pulses converging on Eclipse's most concentrated area. Pain lanced through his twilight form as the pulses disrupted his energy pattern. Eclipse recoiled, flowing along the ceiling to regroup.

The weapons hurt. That was unexpected and concerning.

"Adjusting to frequency pattern Alpha," one operative announced, turning a dial on his weapon. "Fire on my mark."

Eclipse didn't wait for them to coordinate. He dropped from the ceiling directly onto the leader, condensing his twilight form around the man's head and shoulders. The operative stumbled backward, clawing at the twilight energy that obscured his vision and filtered his oxygen.

"Can't... breathe!" the man gasped.

Eclipse felt a moment of remorse. He had no

wish to harm these humans, but Rowan's face flashed in his mind. They hunted her. These people would capture her, experiment on her, just for having been in contact with him. He couldn't allow that.

"Jones is compromised! Switch to pattern Beta!" Another operative adjusted his weapon.

Eclipse released the leader, who collapsed gasping to his knees, and surged toward the new threat. As he moved, a blue pulse caught the edge of his form, sending a shock of disruption through his energy field. Eclipse faltered, his twilight essence momentarily destabilizing.

The Milano operatives pressed their advantage, firing in a coordinated pattern that herded Eclipse against the chamber wall. Each pulse further disrupted his ability to maintain cohesion.

Eclipse needed a new strategy. Changing tactics, he condensed into a more humanoid form and dropped into the underground stream. The cold water interfered with his energy signature, just as it had with Solar's. It was uncomfortable, but it also disrupted the scanners' ability to get a clean lock on him.

"Lost the signal! Spread out!"

Eclipse moved downstream, away from the direction Rowan and Solar had gone. His plan was working, drawing the Milano team away from his companions. But he needed to do more than just distract them temporarily.

He needed to stop them.

Reaching out with his energy field, Eclipse sensed the cave system around him. The rock walls, the flowing water, the subtle vibrations of the Earth itself. An idea formed. Dangerous, possibly devastating, but necessary.

The Milano team was spreading out, sweeping the chamber methodically. Eclipse released a small pulse of energy, just enough to trigger their scanners in his current position. As they converged on him, he reached deep into the rock beneath the stream.

On Zorveya, those from the Twilight Belt rarely used their abilities for destruction. But all energy could be manipulated, even the potential energy stored in Earth's geological formations.

Eclipse sent a focused surge of twilight energy into a fault line running through the cave floor. The rock groaned in protest. Small pebbles skittered down from the ceiling.

"What was that?" One of the operatives looked up nervously.

"Seismic activity," another replied. "These caves are unstable."

"Maintain pursuit," the leader ordered, having recovered enough to rejoin the hunt. "Target Twilight is attempting to escape."

Eclipse sent another pulse, stronger this time, directly into the fault. A crack appeared in the chamber floor, spreading rapidly toward the tunnel Rowan and Solar had taken.

No. He redirected his energy, guiding the fracture away from their escape route and toward the tunnel he'd come through. The ceiling began to crumble in that direction.

"Cave in! Fall back!" The leader shouted, but it was too late.

Eclipse released a final, concentrated burst of twilight energy into the fault line. The effect was immediate and catastrophic. The chamber floor split open with a thunderous crack. Water from the stream poured into the newly formed fissure, creating a whirlpool effect. The ceiling collapsed in sections, blocking the tunnel to the outside.

The Milano operatives scrambled for safety, but the cave-in was too rapid. Two were caught by falling rocks. The others retreated toward the entrance, shouting into their communication devices for backup.

Eclipse felt the strain of such focused energy

manipulation. His twilight form flickered, struggling to maintain cohesion. The geological disruption had cost him more than he'd anticipated.

Yet he couldn't stop now. The cave-in would only delay Milano briefly. He needed to ensure Rowan and Solar had enough time to reach the surface and escape.

Moving through the partially collapsed chamber, Eclipse followed the tunnel Rowan and Solar had taken. His form was weaker now, less substantial, but he pushed forward, determined to verify their safety before considering his own.

A blue pulse of energy struck the wall beside him, one of the Milano operatives had made it through the collapse. Eclipse spun to face the threat, his twilight essence gathering what strength remained.

"Target Twilight is damaged but still mobile," the operative reported into his communicator. "Requesting additional containment teams at junction B."

Eclipse surged forward, engulfing the operative before he could fire again. The man struggled in the twilight field, his weapon discharging wildly. One of the pulses struck Eclipse directly, sending waves of disruption through his already weakened form.

Pain, unlike anything Eclipse had experienced before, tore through his essence. His twilight field began to fragment, losing cohesion. The operative fell to his knees, gasping for air as Eclipse's grip on him weakened.

Eclipse retreated into the tunnel, his form flickering dangerously. Behind him, more Milano personnel poured through the partially collapsed chamber, their scanners beeping as they detected his fading signature.

He needed to reach Rowan. Needed to know she was safe.

The tunnel branched ahead, and Eclipse hesitated. Which way had they gone? His weakened state compromised his ability to sense energy signatures. He chose the path that seemed to lead upward, hoping it would take him to the surface.

As he moved, his twilight essence left fragments behind, small wisps of energy that dissipated into the air. He was losing cohesion rapidly. The weapons had damaged him more severely than he'd realized.

The sound of pursuit grew behind him. Eclipse pushed forward, his consciousness beginning to fragment along with his form. Memories flashed through his mind—the endless negotiations on Zorveya, the crash landing on Earth, and Rowan. Always Rowan, with her remarkable adaptability and the harmony of her energy signature with his own.

The tunnel widened into another chamber, this one with shafts of sunlight streaming from cracks in the ceiling. Eclipse sensed the surface was near. If he could just reach it, perhaps he could find Rowan.

His twilight form surged upward toward the light, but a coordinated barrage of energy pulses struck him from behind. Milano operatives had caught up, their weapons firing in unison.

Eclipse's consciousness shattered into fragments as his twilight essence dispersed throughout the chamber. The last thing he registered was a peculiar containment device being activated beneath him, a swirling vortex of energy that began to draw in the scattered particles of his form.

His final coherent thought was of Rowan. Had she escaped? Was she safe? She was all that mattered.

Then darkness claimed him, and the twilight faded to nothingness.

12

"Don't move," a voice commanded.

From the darkness, a figure materialized, literally flowing out of the shadows like liquid night. Lunar grabbed Rowan by her arm and pulled her to the side. Solar's light illuminated a hole she had almost tripped over.

"Lunar," Solar growled, his form brightening again. "Where have you been while we fought for our lives?"

"Observing," Lunar replied coolly. "And preparing an escape route." He turned his night-dark eyes to Rowan. "Where is Eclipse?"

The question hit her like a physical blow. "He stayed behind to hold them off."

Something shifted in Lunar's expression.

Concern, perhaps? Though it was difficult to read emotions on his shadowy features.

"Milano has deployed energy-dampening technology," Solar explained. "They found us at the Desert Suite and attacked in force."

"I am aware," Lunar said. "Poppy and I witnessed their deployment from the canyon rim. She's securing transportation while I tracked your energy signatures to find you." His gaze returned to Rowan. "You left a rather obvious trail."

"I'm sorry I don't have shadow-walking powers," Rowan snapped, her fear for Eclipse making her irritable. She started to turn back, but another distant rumble shook the cave, this one weaker than before.

"We must keep moving," Lunar urged. "An exit suitable to your dimensions is this way."

He led them through a series of increasingly narrow passages, at times seeming to merge with the shadows completely. Rowan struggled to keep up, her wet clothes heavy and her muscles aching from the cold and exertion.

"Wait," she gasped as they climbed a particularly steep section. "I need to catch my breath."

"There is no time," Lunar insisted. "Milano's forces are deploying throughout the canyon. They have devices that flash with light when they detect our energy signatures."

"Energy scanners," Rowan mumbled to herself. "Like the ones they used to find us at the retreat."

"Precisely," Lunar confirmed. "We must reach Poppy's vehicle before they establish a perimeter."

Solar helped Rowan up a particularly difficult section, his touch leaving her skin tingling with residual energy.

"What about Eclipse?" she insisted again. "We can't just leave him."

"Eclipse is capable of defending himself," Lunar said, though his tone lacked conviction. "And he would prioritize the mission over his individual safety."

"This isn't a mission anymore," Rowan argued. "This is survival."

"Same objective, different terminology," Solar said.

The aliens' dry, matter-of-fact personality traits were more annoying when coming from these two.

They climbed in silence for several minutes before emerging into a narrow crevice where natural light streamed down from above. Lunar pointed to a series of handholds carved into the rock face.

"This leads to the surface," he explained. "Poppy

will be waiting with transportation approximately half a kilometer north of the exit point."

Rowan took a deep breath as she looked up. This was not going to be fun.

She began the ascent, her arms trembling with fatigue. The climb seemed endless, each handhold requiring more effort than the last. Just as her strength was about to give out, a human hand reached down from above.

Poppy's face appeared at the opening, her expression a mix of concern and determination.

"Hurry," she urged. "Helicopters are coming back around."

With a final effort, Rowan pulled herself out of the crevice and onto the sun-baked red rock of the canyon rim. Solar emerged next, his golden form immediately dimming to avoid detection. Lunar flowed up last, barely distinguishable from the shadows cast by the rocks.

"Where's Eclipse?" Poppy asked, noticing the missing alien.

Rowan was really tired of that question. None of them seemed worried whenever she told them what happened.

"Still in the caves," Rowan said, her voice tight. "He stayed behind to fight off Milano."

Poppy's eyes widened. "We need to go back for him. No one gets left behind."

Finally!

"No time," Lunar said, pointing skyward.

A black helicopter appeared over the canyon ridge, its rotors slicing through the desert air. Below it, dust clouds rose from multiple vehicles traversing the off-road trails.

"They're preparing to flush us out," Lunar observed.

"This way," Poppy urged, leading them toward a cluster of boulders where an ancient jeep was hidden.

"That's your transportation?" Solar asked skeptically.

"It's better than walking," Poppy shot back. "And it knows these trails better than any fancy SUV."

They piled in, Rowan in the passenger seat with Poppy driving, the aliens squeezed in the back. Poppy threw a silver blanket over the guys. The jeep roared to life, its engine loud in the canyon's quiet.

"What about Dani?" Rowan asked. "She was supposed to warn you about the attack."

"We found her in the caves looking for you," Poppy explained, throwing the jeep into gear. "She escaped the retreat in an alien flash mob of all things.

She's meeting us at the rendezvous point with supplies."

The jeep lurched forward, bouncing over the rugged terrain. Poppy drove with surprising skill, navigating between rock formations and along barely visible trails.

"Where are we going?" Rowan asked, clinging to the roll bar as they hit a particularly rough patch.

"Off-grid cabin," Poppy replied. "About twenty miles into the backcountry. No electricity, no cell service, definitely no non-biological thermal signatures for them to track."

The helicopter appeared again, sweeping low over the canyon. Poppy immediately swerved under an overhanging rock formation, cutting the engine.

"Down," she hissed.

They huddled in the jeep as the helicopter passed overhead, its shadow sliding over the rocks. Rowan held her breath, expecting to hear shots or see troops rappelling down at any moment. But the helicopter continued on, apparently not spotting them.

"They're scanning for energy signatures, not vehicles," Lunar observed. "Solar and I must minimize our emissions."

"Stay under that silver blanket," Poppy ordered.

Solar grimaced, his form dimming further until

he was barely brighter than a human. "This is uncomfortable."

"Maintaining physical form without full energy expression is difficult," Lunar agreed, his own shadow form condensing into something more humanoid.

Poppy waited until the helicopter was well past before restarting the jeep and continuing their escape.

As they bounced along the trail, Rowan kept looking back toward the caves, hoping to see a familiar twilight form emerging from the rocks. Nothing.

"He'll find us," Poppy said, noticing Rowan's backward glances. "Eclipse strikes me as the type who always finds a way."

Rowan nodded, not trusting herself to speak. The cold, wet clothes, the adrenaline crash, and the fear for Eclipse were all catching up with her. She shivered despite the desert heat.

The jeep rounded a bend and descended into a dry wash, forcing Poppy to slow down. The trail here was barely discernible, marked only by subtle differences in the rock coloration.

"There," Lunar said suddenly, pointing ahead.

A figure stood in the middle of the wash, waving urgently. Dani.

Poppy pulled up beside her, and Dani immediately climbed in, squeezing into the back with the aliens.

"Thank god you made it," she said breathlessly. "Milano teams are swarming everywhere." She looked around. "Where's Eclipse?"

The question hung in the air, unanswered but for a slight shake of Poppy's head.

"We need to keep moving," Lunar said after a moment. "Milano will expand their search perimeter once they realize we've escaped the caves."

Poppy nodded and accelerated down the wash, following it until it joined a slightly more established jeep trail.

"I've got water, food, and some basic first aid in my pack," Dani offered, passing a water bottle to Rowan. "And we managed to grab these from the suite."

She pulled out a small metal object that Rowan recognized as Eclipse's energy stone, along with a few other alien devices.

"How did you know to take these?" Solar asked, surprised.

"I figured they might be important," Dani explained. "When Milano started closing in, one of Rowan's alien enthusiast friends figured they shouldn't get their hands on any more alien tech. They gave it to me for safekeeping."

Rowan took the energy stone, cradling it in her palm. It hummed faintly, almost as if responding to her touch.

"Can we use this to contact him?" she asked.

"Possibly," Solar replied. "The energy stones are attuned to their owners. It might respond to Eclipse's signature if he's within range."

Rowan held the stone tightly, willing it to connect with Eclipse, to show some sign he was still out there. The stone remained inert, its soft hum unchanged.

"We'll try again when we're settled," Poppy reassured her. "Right now, we need to focus on getting to safety."

The jeep continued its jarring journey across the backcountry, gradually leaving the more traveled areas behind. The terrain became increasingly rugged, the trail sometimes disappearing entirely before reappearing hundreds of yards later.

"How much further?" Solar asked, his form flickering slightly with each major bump.

"About five more miles," Poppy answered. "We'll be there before sunset."

Rowan stared out at the passing landscape, the

red rocks and scrubby vegetation blurring together. Her thoughts kept returning to Eclipse—his twilight energy expanding to protect her, his voice urging her to continue without him.

Had it only been this morning that she'd awakened in his arms, feeling more connected than she ever had to another being?

And now he was gone, possibly captured by Milano, all because she'd suggested that ridiculous reconnaissance mission.

"This is my fault," she said quietly. "We should never have left the suite."

"No," Solar responded firmly. "Milano was already tracking us. They would have found us regardless."

"Solar is correct," Lunar added. "Their technology is advanced. They were hunting us systematically."

"Which brings us back to how they got that technology in the first place," Dani pointed out. "I mean, energy weapons specifically designed to counter alien powers? That's not something they developed overnight."

"The missing Milano founder," Rowan remembered suddenly. "Darren reminded me of the rumors that Milano's founder disappeared after claiming aliens had abducted him."

"Perhaps not a claim," Lunar suggested. "Perhaps fact."

But none of that really mattered right now. The fact was Milano had the tech and they were hunting aliens.

The implications hung heavy in the air as the jeep bounced onward, deeper into the wilderness, the sun sinking lower toward the horizon, casting the red rocks in deepening shades of crimson and purple.

Twilight was approaching. Eclipse's time.

Rowan clutched the energy stone tighter, whispering into it, "Find us. Please feel me and find us."

13

Consciousness returned to Eclipse in fragments. They were disconnected sensations and impressions rather than coherent thoughts. First came awareness of containment, a sense of being compressed into a space too small for his natural form. Then, pain radiated through what remained of his energy field. Finally, he was conscious of his surroundings, although still without visual perception.

He attempted to expand his twilight essence to reestablish his form, but encountered resistance. There was a pulsing barrier of energy that pushed back against his efforts, maintaining his compression.

An energy-dampening field. Sophisticated. Far

beyond what Earth technology should be capable of generating.

What was this trip Galaxy Alien Mail Order Brides had taken them on?

Eclipse focused inward, assessing his condition. Milano's weapons had severely fragmented his essence, and portions of his energy pattern were disrupted. What remained felt depleted, barely sufficient to maintain consciousness, let alone attempt escape.

How long had he been contained? Without access to external stimuli, time was impossible to measure.

Rowan. Had she escaped? Was she safe?

The thought of her galvanized what remained of his strength. Eclipse pushed against the containment field again, searching for any weakness, any fluctuation he might exploit. The barrier flared in response, sending waves of disruption through his essence that forced him to retreat.

A mechanical sound penetrated his awareness, followed by a door opening and footsteps approaching.

"Containment field holding at eighty-seven percent capacity," a clinical voice stated. "Subject shows increased activity when probed but remains securely confined."

"Remarkable," another voice responded, this one familiar. James Petersen. "The energy signature is unlike anything we've recorded before. Neither purely light-based like Subject Solar nor shadow-based like the unidentified third entity."

"'Twilight," a third voice corrected, deeper and more authoritative than the others. "We're designating this one Eclipse. That was the name we heard used by the woman. The readings suggest it exists in a state between energy and matter, a form of twilight manifestation."

Eclipse struggled to gather his scattered essence, trying desperately to form something resembling eyes. The effort was agony, but he managed to create just enough awareness to make out three blurry human shapes standing in front of the glowing cylinder that imprisoned him. His prison. His cage.

"Can it understand us?" the authoritative voice asked.

"Unknown," Petersen replied. "But the energy pattern shows responsiveness to auditory stimuli. There's intelligence there, certainly."

The authoritative figure stepped closer to the containment field. Eclipse could see him more clearly. He was an older human male with silver hair and a bearing that suggested command.

"I am Director Malcolm Vega of Milano Enterprises Special Projects Division," he stated, addressing Eclipse directly. "We know what you are. We know there are more of you. If you cooperate, your treatment will improve."

Eclipse remained silent, conserving his strength. Even if he could form words, revealing his communication abilities would provide them with valuable information.

"Still playing inert?" Vega smiled thinly. "No matter. The energy dampeners will keep you contained while we analyze your composition. Your companions will join you soon enough."

Companions. They hadn't captured the others yet. Relief surged through him, causing a momentary flare in his energy pattern that registered on the monitors surrounding his containment unit.

"Interesting response," the technician noted. "Elevated energy output when companions are mentioned."

"Make a note," Vega ordered. "We'll exploit that emotional connection later if necessary."

Vega turned to leave, then paused. "Increase the containment field to ninety-five percent capacity. I don't want any surprises from this one. The last alien who thought it could outsmart us provided valuable technology, but the cost was substantial."

The technician adjusted controls on a panel, and Eclipse felt the compression intensify. His consciousness began to fragment again under the increased pressure.

"Sir," Petersen hesitated, "what about the human woman? She was clearly involved with these entities."

"Find her," Vega replied. "She might be useful in securing cooperation from our guest here. But our priority is to contain the other two energy beings. Especially the solar one. His power signature could revolutionize our energy technology. Think of the money we'd save if we hooked him up to a power grid."

The three men exited the laboratory, leaving Eclipse alone in his cylindrical prison. As the door sealed shut, the lights dimmed to a low blue glow that pulsed in rhythm with the containment field. Eclipse allowed what remained of his consciousness to drift, conserving strength while assessing his condition.

His twilight essence was severely compromised. The weapons Milano deployed had been specifically calibrated to disrupt energy-based lifeforms, fragmenting his cohesion at the quantum level. In his home zone on Zorveya, surrounded by the natural twilight energies, recovery would have been swift. Here, trapped in this dampening field, regeneration was painfully slow.

Time passed. Eclipse had no way to measure it precisely. The laboratory remained empty for the most part, although technicians entered to adjust settings and take readings. They never spoke directly to him, discussing him as if he were merely an interesting specimen.

"Subject maintains a cohesive field despite fragmentation," one noted. "Remarkable resilience compared to the Bevlonian we processed last year."

"Different energy pattern entirely," another replied. "The twilight signature shows properties of both absorption and emission. Neither fully light nor shadow."

Bevlonian. The word registered in Eclipse's fragmented consciousness. A species from the Omega quadrant, notorious for their aggressive territorial expansion. Had Milano encountered them before? Had they captured one?

This confirmed what Eclipse had suspected. Milano had prior experience with extraterrestrial beings. Their technology was too advanced, too specifically tailored to be the result of theoretical research alone.

Eclipse forced himself to remain passive, to reveal nothing of his intelligence or comprehension. Every piece of information they gleaned from him would be weaponized against Solar and Lunar. Against Rowan.

Rowan. Her name rippled through his essence, creating a momentary surge that registered on the monitoring equipment. A technician made note of it, but thankfully didn't seem to understand the cause.

Eclipse retreated deeper into himself, focusing on the connection he had formed with her. Their resonance had been unprecedented, a harmonic convergence that transcended normal energy interactions. If any trace of that connection remained, perhaps he could use it.

The pain of containment faded as Eclipse concentrated on the memory of Rowan's energy signature, the unique rhythm of her human bioelectrical field. He had never attempted to form a connection across distance before. On Zorveya, such abilities were theoretical at best, the subject of ancient legends rather than scientific study.

But desperate circumstances required desperate measures.

Eclipse gathered what remained of his fragmented essence, concentrating it into a focused pulse attuned to the specific frequency of Rowan's energy pattern. The effort was agonizing, like tearing apart what little cohesion he had managed to maintain.

The containment field flared in response, tightening around him. Alarms blared. The door burst open as technicians rushed in.

"Containment surge. Energy spike in Subject Eclipse!"

"Increase damping field to maximum!"

The pressure intensified unbearably, but Eclipse had already released his pulse. A microscopic fragment of his twilight essence, encoded with his consciousness, projected outward through the quantum field. Whether it would reach Rowan, whether she could even receive it, he couldn't know.

The effort had cost him dearly. Eclipse's consciousness began to dissolve under the increased pressure of the containment field. His form collapsed inward, no longer able to maintain even the barest semblance of structure.

The last thing he registered before perception failed entirely was a technician's voice, "Subject showing critical destabilization. Alert Director Vega immediately."

Darkness claimed him, deeper than any he had known before.

ECLIPSE DRIFTED IN A VOID, neither conscious nor unconscious. Time had no meaning. His essence existed in a state of suspended animation, prevented from dissolution by the containment field yet unable to regenerate.

Occasionally, awareness would flicker briefly, snippets of conversation, the sensation of being moved, sharp bursts of pain as his energy was sampled and analyzed. But these moments were disconnected, impossible to organize into a coherent timeline.

"...molecular resonance suggests an entirely different evolutionary path..."

"...energy conversion efficiency exceeding ninety-seven percent..."

"...subject remains unresponsive to stimuli..."

"...prepare for phase two testing..."

In these brief moments of semi-consciousness, Eclipse focused on a single thought, a name that anchored what remained of his identity. Rowan.

Rowan.

Rowan.

Had she escaped the caves? Had his sacrifice been worthwhile? Were Solar and Lunar still free? These questions circled endlessly without answers.

During a brief period of increased lucidity, Eclipse became aware that he was no longer in the same laboratory. The energy signature of the containment field had changed, becoming more sophisticated. The space around him felt larger, designed for more extensive testing.

"Director Vega, the subject has been successfully transferred to the primary research facility," a voice reported. "Initial molecular mapping is complete."

"Excellent." Vega's voice was unmistakable. "And the progress on locating the others?"

"Still negative, sir. The desert terrain makes tracking difficult, especially with their ability to mask energy signatures. But we've established checkpoints on all major roads leaving Duskrock."

"Unacceptable. I want the search parameters expanded. Bring in the orbital scanner if necessary."

"Sir, that would require authorization from—"

"I'll handle the authorization. Those entities represent the most significant scientific discovery since our first contact event. I will not lose them due to bureaucratic timidity."

The voices faded as Eclipse's awareness dimmed again. But a new thought had formed. They hadn't found the others yet. His sacrifice had bought them time. Perhaps they had reached safety. Maybe they had even gone home.

Home.

Rowan.

More time passed in the void. Eclipse felt his twilight essence slowly begin to regenerate, as the natural processes of his physiology adapted to work within the constraints of the containment field. It wasn't enough to escape, not nearly enough to challenge the sophisticated technology surrounding him, but it was something.

With this minimal regeneration came greater awareness of his surroundings. Eclipse could now perceive that he was contained within a specialized chamber filled with various analytical devices. He was not the only specimen. Other containment fields housed objects of alien origin, though none appeared to contain living entities.

During one testing session, Eclipse heard something that triggered a surge of fear.

"Sir, we've detected an unusual energy fluctuation in the desert sector, approximately twenty miles northwest of the original contact site."

"Show me," Vega demanded.

A holographic display flickered to life, showing a topographical map with a pulsing indicator.

"It's faint, sir. Intermittent. But the signature bears similarities to our captured subject."

"Twilight energy?" Vega leaned closer to the display.

"Not exactly. It's like an echo, or a resonance pattern. Almost as if something is responding to our subject here. I think they may be talking to each other."

Eclipse felt a jolt of recognition. His energy stone. It had to be. If Rowan had it, if she was trying to use it... That meant she got his message.

"Deploy a reconnaissance team immediately," Vega ordered. "Minimal personnel, maximum stealth. I want confirmation before we commit resources."

"Yes, sir. And the subject?"

Vega turned toward Eclipse's containment field. Though Eclipse couldn't see his expression clearly, he sensed the human's assessment.

"Prepare it for transport to Sector 7. If this is what I think it is, we may need our guest as leverage."

Eclipse forced himself to remain passive, to show no reaction that might register on their instruments. Inside, however, his essence surged with renewed purpose. If Milano was detecting his energy stone, it meant Rowan not only had it but was attempting to use it. Perhaps even trying to find him.

It had to be her. Solar and Lunar would never try to find him that way.

For the first time since his capture, Eclipse allowed himself to experience something dangerous: hope.

But also, still fear.

Rowan could be in danger.

As technicians prepared to move his containment unit, Eclipse focused all his awareness on gathering his strength. Milano believed him to be incapacitated, barely conscious. Let them maintain that belief. Let them underestimate what remained of his abilities.

They had studied his energy patterns, but they didn't understand what motivated them. They didn't comprehend the power of the connection he shared with Rowan, a quantum entanglement that transcended physical distance.

Eclipse retreated into the deepest part of his consciousness, to where the essence of his true self remained uncompromised. There, he nurtured a small, hidden spark, a reservoir of twilight energy shielded from Milano's detection.

Rowan was out there. She was searching for him. And when the moment came, he would be ready.

The containment field hummed as it was prepared for transport. Eclipse allowed himself to drift again, conserving strength for whatever came next. His last coherent thought before returning to the void was simple but profound.

Rowan. I am here, waiting in the twilight between worlds.

14

Rowan's knuckles were white against the worn leather of the jeep steering wheel as she navigated the rugged desert trail. The vehicle bounced violently over ruts and stones, but she didn't slow down. She couldn't. Not with Eclipse's energy stone pulsing against her chest, tucked safely in a makeshift pouch she'd fashioned from a strip of leather and hung around her neck.

"I'm coming," she whispered, as if he could hear her. "Just hold on."

The stone had changed three hours ago. After days of silence, three endless days of hopelessness, it had suddenly warmed against her skin in the predawn darkness, emanating a faint purple glow that matched the twilight color of Eclipse's true form.

That's when she knew. He was alive, and some-how, he was calling to her.

She could find him.

The desert stretched endlessly before her, red rocks and scrub brush blurring as tears pricked at her eyes. She'd left the cabin before sunrise, stealing away while Lunar was distracted and Poppy was still asleep. She'd left a note, of course. She wasn't completely reckless.

"Gone to find Eclipse. Milano has him. Don't follow. Stay hidden. I'll be back."

She hoped it was true.

Rowan had taken Poppy's jeep and snuck away without asking. Lunar needed to remain hidden. Two strange aliens named Bob and Gary had picked up Solar and Dani. The aliens had contacted them through a communication device that looked like a tiny drone, explaining that extraction had become too dangerous with Milano's increased surveillance.

They'd managed to get Solar and Dani safely aboard their ship under cover of darkness, but Eclipse's energy signature was missing from their scanners.

She hadn't mentioned how she knew where to find Eclipse.

"We'll return for the others in fourteen Earth

days," Bob had told Lunar. "Once Milano gives up their hunt."

Fourteen days. Two weeks of Milano having Eclipse. It was too long. She couldn't wait. Not when she felt him. Galaxy Brides was an all but useless ally. Their extraction timelines seemed arbitrarily set. First a month. Then forty-eight hours. Now fourteen days.

The stone pulsed again, stronger this time. Rowan adjusted her course slightly, following its rhythmic response like an otherworldly compass. The closer she got, the more intensely it vibrated.

According to the tattered map she'd found in Poppy's glove compartment, she was approaching an area marked with nothing but a series of hash marks and a warning, *"Gov't Land. No Trespassing."*

Precisely where she'd expect a secret Milano research facility to be located.

The terrain grew increasingly rougher as she followed a barely visible track that wound between massive red rock formations. The jeep's ancient suspension groaned in protest.

"Come on, baby. Just a little farther," she coaxed the vehicle, patting its dashboard like a faithful pet.

The sun had risen, casting long shadows across the desert floor. She'd have to abandon the jeep soon and continue on foot. A vehicle this noisy would alert any security patrols long before she got close enough to do Eclipse any good.

As she rounded a bend, a massive mesa rose before her, its flat top perfect for concealing a facility. The energy stone practically hummed against her skin now, confirmation she was on the right track.

Rowan brought the jeep to a stop behind a large boulder and cut the engine. She sat for a moment in the sudden silence, listening for any signs she'd been detected. There was nothing but the whisper of desert wind and the hard beating of her heart.

She'd be lying if she said she wasn't scared. She was terrified.

Rowan checked her supplies. There was a backpack containing water, power bars, a first aid kit, binoculars, and a small toolkit she'd found in Poppy's cabin. Hardly the equipment needed for a rescue mission, but it was all she had.

A gun would have been better. Or an army.

She didn't want to face this alone, but Eclipse needed her.

The stone pulsed again, more urgently.

"I know," she whispered. "I'm hurrying."

Rowan secured the backpack, tucked her hair under a baseball cap, and set out on foot. The desert heat pressed down on her as she climbed the rocky slope that led toward the mesa. Every few minutes, she paused to scan her surroundings with the binoculars, watching for security patrols and surveillance equipment.

After what felt like at least an hour into her climb, she spotted a glint of metal where there should be only stone. Rowan pressed into hiding, breathing deeply.

She redefined her path, picking a safer route. As she drew closer, the outline of a facility emerged, partially built into the mesa itself. Solar panels covered one section of the roof, with satellite dishes and antennas clustered nearby. A perimeter fence surrounded the complex, with guard stations positioned at regular intervals.

Rowan found a sheltered position behind a rocky outcrop and studied the facility through her binoculars. The main entrance appeared to be on the east side, with a checkpoint for vehicles. Smaller personnel doors were located around the perimeter, all of which required key card access, as indicated by the scanner panels mounted beside them.

"Great," she muttered. "Just walk up and knock, I guess?"

The stone against her chest grew suddenly hot,

almost painfully so. Rowan gasped and pulled it from beneath her shirt. It glowed with an intensity she hadn't seen before, pulsing in a distinct pattern that couldn't be natural.

Three short pulses. Three long. Three short again. Over and over.

"S.O.S.," she realized aloud. "Eclipse, are you... Can you hear me?"

The stone's rhythm changed immediately, as if in response to her voice. It wasn't just leading her to him. It was communicating.

Rowan closed her eyes and concentrated, wrapping her fingers around the stone. "I'm here," she whispered. "I'm coming for you. Just tell me how to get in."

The stone grew warmer, and images suddenly flashed through Rowan's mind. They were fragmented and chaotic, but recognizable.

A ventilation shaft on the facility's western side.

A service entrance with a single guard.

A schedule for patrol rotations.

"Eclipse," she gasped. "Are you showing me this?"

The stone pulsed once, and she felt more than heard the answer. *Yes.*

Rowan's heart raced. Somehow, Eclipse was able to communicate through their connection. The quantum harmonic convergence he'd talked about wasn't just fancy alien talk for attraction. It was a real, tangible link between them.

"Show me again," she urged. "Show me the best way in."

The images returned, clearer this time.

A service entrance on the northwest corner of the facility.

Guard changes at specific intervals.

A maintenance worker left his key card on a break room table.

Rowan committed everything to memory, then checked her watch. If Eclipse's intelligence was correct, she had forty minutes before the next guard rotation. This was her best chance to approach undetected.

She used the time to circle around to the northwest side of the facility, staying low and using the terrain for cover. The desert had taught her patience during her months in Duskrock, and now she drew on that lesson, moving methodically, never rushing despite the urgent pull of the stone against her skin.

When she reached a position overlooking the service entrance, Rowan settled in to observe. Just as Eclipse had shown her, a single guard stood at the door, looking bored and uncomfortable in the desert heat. Every few minutes, he checked his watch as if counting down to the end of his shift.

At precisely the time Eclipse had indicated, a second guard emerged from the building to relieve the first. There was a brief exchange, a clipboard passed between them, and then the first guard disappeared back inside.

The new guard immediately pulled out his phone, attention diverted. "Hey, hon, Director Vega needs us to stay late tonight. Yeah, I know, but what the big boss wants..."

This was her window.

Rowan crept closer, using a drainage ditch that ran near the fence line for cover. When she was within fifty yards of the entrance, she removed her backpack and left it hidden behind a rock. She would move faster without it, and if everything went wrong, it would be waiting for her escape... assuming she made it that far.

She kept only the stone, which still pulsed with Eclipse's presence, and a small multi-tool from Poppy's kit. Not much of a weapon, but better than nothing.

Twenty yards from the fence, Rowan froze as a patrol vehicle rounded the corner of the building. She pressed herself flat against the earth, hardly daring to breathe as the vehicle passed slowly along the perimeter. Once it disappeared around the far side, she continued her approach.

The fence was her first real obstacle, with ten feet of chain link topped with razor wire. But Eclipse had shown her something else, a place where the earth had eroded beneath the fence, creating a gap just barely wide enough for a person to squeeze through.

Rowan found it exactly where he'd indicated, partially concealed by a clump of desert brush. She lay flat and began to wriggle beneath the fence, ignoring the sharp stones that dug into her skin and the metal links that snagged her clothing.

Halfway through, she caught the back of her shirt on the fence. The slight noise made the guard glance up from his phone. Rowan froze.

After what felt like an eternity, the guard returned his attention to his screen. Rowan carefully disentangled herself and finished squeezing through the gap.

Now inside the perimeter, she stayed low, using the scattered maintenance equipment for cover as she approached the building. The service door was just several feet away, requiring a key card she didn't have.

The stone pulsed against her skin, three rapid beats followed by a pause, then three more. Rowan understood. She needed to wait.

Three minutes later, a maintenance worker emerged, a cigarette already between his lips. He propped the door open with a small rock and moved a few paces away to light up, his back to the entrance.

Rowan didn't hesitate. She darted forward, keeping the worker between herself and the guard, and slipped through the open door. She was in.

The corridor beyond was dimly lit and utilitarian, lined with pipes and electrical conduits. Rowan pressed herself against the wall, listening for any sign she'd been detected. The stone grew warmer against her skin, pulsing in a different pattern like a kind of directional guidance.

"Left," she whispered, interpreting its signals. "Then right at the junction."

She followed the stone's guidance through a maze of service corridors, occasionally ducking into doorways or maintenance closets when footsteps approached. The facility was larger than it had appeared from outside, much of it extending deep into the mesa itself.

The pulse of the stone grew stronger, more insistent as she descended a metal staircase to a lower level. The air here was cooler, with the distinct hum of advanced equipment. Signs on the walls warned of restricted areas and security protocols.

Rowan rounded a corner and nearly collided with a woman in a lab coat. Both froze in surprise.

"You're not authorized to be here," the scientist said, reaching for an ID badge that presumably contained an alarm.

Rowan reacted on instinct. "Actually, I am," she said with all the confidence she could muster. "Director Vega sent me to check on the twilight subject. There's been an energy fluctuation."

The scientist's hand hesitated. "I wasn't informed—"

"It just happened," Rowan interrupted. "He's waiting for my report. You can call him if you want, but you know how he gets when he's kept waiting."

It was a gamble, but one based on the fragments of information she'd gleaned from Eclipse's communications. The scientist's expression shifted from suspicion to uncertainty.

"Fine," she said finally. "But you'll need to sign in at the security station."

"Already did," Rowan lied smoothly. "Look, just point me to Containment Lab 7, and I'll get out of your hair."

The scientist's eyes narrowed. "Lab 7?"

Rowan's heart sank. Wrong guess. But before she could backpedal, the stone against her chest grew searingly hot, and words seemed to form in her mind, Eclipse's voice clearer than she'd ever heard it.

"*Sector 7. Not Lab 7. Authorization code 25-Twilight-9.*"

"Sorry, long day. Sector 7," Rowan corrected. "Authorization code 25-Twilight-9."

The scientist relaxed slightly. "Through those doors, then take the elevator to sublevel three. You'll need your access card."

"Got it right here," Rowan patted her pocket. "Thanks."

She walked confidently in the direction indicated, feeling the scientist's eyes on her back. The moment she passed through the doors, she broke into a run. That bluff wouldn't hold for long. The scientist would check, find no record of her authorization, and sound the alarm.

The elevator required a key card, but Eclipse was ahead of her again. The stone showed her an image of a maintenance override panel hidden behind a decorative wall plate. Rowan used Poppy's multi-tool to pry open the panel, and followed the sequence of button presses Eclipse showed her.

The elevator hummed to life, descending to sublevel three without requiring any credentials. As the doors opened, the stone pulsed so strongly it seemed to be trying to pull itself from around her neck.

"Close now. Hurry. They know."

An alarm began to wail somewhere above her. Her bluff had been called.

Rowan sprinted down the corridor, following the stone's pull. The hallway opened into a large laboratory filled with complex equipment. And there, in the center of the room, was a glowing cylindrical containment unit.

Inside, a swirling mass of purple-blue energy pulsed weakly.

"Eclipse!" Rowan rushed to the cylinder, pressing her hands against its glass-like surface. "I'm here. I'm going to get you out."

The twilight essence within shifted, forming a semblance of Eclipse's face against the barrier where her hands touched.

"Control panel. Hurry."

Rowan spotted the control console nearby. It was complex, with dozens of switches and readouts monitoring Eclipse's containment.

"Which buttons?" she asked desperately, hearing footsteps approaching.

The stone guided her hands to specific controls. None of them meant anything to her.

"Um, power regulators, containment field generator, emergency release protocols." She hesitated. "Eclipse, this is going to trigger every alarm they have."

"Already detected. No choice."

"Right." Rowan took a deep breath and began the shutdown sequence that Eclipse showed her. Warning messages flashed across the screens. Automated voices announced containment field failures.

The door to the lab burst open. James Petersen stood there, flanked by security personnel with weapons drawn.

"Step away from the controls, Ms. Clark," he ordered.

"Sorry, Jimmy. Not happening." Rowan slammed her hand down on the emergency release, then grabbed the stone from around her neck and pressed it against the containment field.

The effect was instantaneous and spectacular. The stone shattered in her hand, releasing a burst of twilight energy that merged with Eclipse's essence. The containment field collapsed in a shower of electrical discharges. Alarms screamed from every corner of the lab.

Eclipse's twilight form surged outward, expanding rapidly to fill the room. The security personnel fired their weapons, but the energy pulses passed harmlessly through his diffused essence.

Petersen backed toward the door. "Containment breach! Seal the facility!"

Eclipse's twilight energy coalesced around Rowan, enveloping her in a protective cocoon of purple-blue light. His voice resonated within her mind, clearer than ever.

"*Hold onto me.*"

Rowan felt herself lifting off the ground as Eclipse's energy field intensified around her. The sensation was familiar. It was the same resonance they'd shared during their night together, but magnified a hundredfold. Her body tingled as her biorhythms synchronized with his energy patterns.

"What are you doing?" she gasped.

"*Trust me.*"

She did. Wholeheartedly.

Eclipse's twilight form surged toward the ceiling, taking her with him. Security personnel continued firing uselessly as Eclipse's essence simply flowed around the energy pulses.

"The ventilation system," Petersen shouted. "Seal the ducts!"

But Eclipse was already flowing into the air circulation system, carrying Rowan like air with him. She felt simultaneously solid and insubstantial, her physical form partially merged with his energy field. It should have been terrifying, but instead it felt right, as if this was how they were always meant to be.

They traveled through the narrow ducts at impossible speed, Eclipse's twilight essence adapting to each twist and turn. Rowan could sense his thoughts, fragmented but determined.

"Surface. Freedom. Together."

Ahead, light filtered through a vent grating. Eclipse's energy surged toward it, breaking through the metal barrier and erupting into the open desert air. They emerged on the facility's roof, momentarily free but far from safe.

Eclipse reformed into a more humanoid shape, still holding Rowan close within his energy field. She could see the facility mobilizing beneath them. The security personnel poured out of the doors, starting up vehicles as weapons were being deployed.

"We need to run," she urged.

"Can't run. Too weak. But can fly."

Eclipse's form expanded again, becoming less defined, more like the twilight sky itself. Rowan felt herself growing lighter as her body harmonized further with his essence.

"Eclipse, what are you—"

"Trust me."

How could she not? Their connection had transcended physical boundaries from the first moment they'd touched. Now, Eclipse was taking that connection to its logical conclusion... a complete harmonic convergence.

15

Eclipse had never attempted anything like this before. As his twilight essence expanded around Rowan, he felt her consciousness merging with his own, not completely, but enough that their energies resonated in perfect synchronicity. Her human form remained distinct within his twilight field, yet they moved as one entity, flowing through air ducts and rising above the Milano facility into the clear desert sky.

Below them, chaos erupted. Security personnel poured from the building, weapons aimed upward. Energy pulses flashed through the air, but Eclipse twisted his essence around Rowan, shielding her from harm. Each pulse that struck him sent ripples of pain through his already weakened form, but he maintained cohesion through sheer determination.

Must protect Rowan. Must escape.

The thought reverberated through their shared consciousness. Eclipse felt Rowan's response, not in words, but in emotions. At the core of them, she felt concern for his condition, and something deeper that resonated with his own feelings for her.

Humans had a word for it. Love.

"They're coming after us," Rowan's voice reached him, both through conventional sound and through their connection. She gestured toward black helicopters lifting off from a hidden hangar on the far side of the facility.

Eclipse focused his remaining strength, pushing them higher and faster across the desert landscape. He had never traveled this way on Zorveya. Twilight energy was meant for balance and mediation, not rapid movement. But necessity had taught him much during his time on Earth, expanding his understanding of his own abilities.

"Mesa... to the west... cover..."

His thoughts were becoming fragmented, his energy reserves dangerously low after days of containment. The effort of maintaining their flight while protecting Rowan threatened to deplete him entirely.

"I see it," Rowan replied, somehow understanding his broken communication. "That outcropping. Can you make it?"

Eclipse surged forward, his twilight field streaming behind them like the aurora of Earth's polar regions. He sensed Rowan's wonder at the experience of semi-corporeal flight.

The helicopters gained ground, equipped with spotlights that swept the terrain. One beam caught them momentarily, and Eclipse felt the distinctive signature of an energy scanner as it activated. He twisted sharply, diving toward a narrow ravine that cut through the desert floor.

The sudden maneuver sent fresh pain cascading through his essence, and Eclipse felt his cohesion wavering. Rowan sensed it immediately.

"You're hurting. You need to set us down."

"*Not... safe yet...*"

"Eclipse, please," she begged. "You're burning yourself out. I can feel it."

She was right. The rescue and flight had depleted his already diminished reserves. However, the Milano pursuit was relentless, with the helicopters closing in despite his evasive maneuvers.

As they approached the mesa, Eclipse detected a familiar energy signature, faint but recognizable, emanating from a small structure nestled against the rock face.

"I see them... Lunar..."

"What? Lunar?" Rowan strained to see where he indicated.

Eclipse adjusted their course, heading for the rough cabin barely visible against the red rocks. As they drew closer, a figure emerged from the shadows. He recognized the unmistakable darkness-absorbing form of Lunar.

With a final surge of strength, Eclipse carried them the remaining distance, his twilight field collapsing as they reached the cabin's perimeter. They tumbled to the ground, Eclipse's essence barely maintaining humanoid shape as Rowan rolled free.

"Eclipse!" She scrambled to his side, her hands passing through his unstable form.

Lunar moved swiftly to them, his shadow essence reaching out to Eclipse's flickering twilight energy.

"He is severely depleted," Lunar observed, his normally detached tone carrying an edge of concern.

"Help him," Rowan pleaded, looking up as the helicopter searchlights swept closer.

"Inside," Lunar ordered, his shadow-form

expanding to help gather Eclipse's dissipating essence. "The structure is shielded."

Together, they brought Eclipse into the small cabin where Poppy waited.

"What happened to him?" Poppy demanded, securing the door behind them.

"Milano," Rowan answered. "They had him in some kind of energy containment. He broke free but used everything he had to get us here."

Eclipse tried to focus and re-form his essence into something more substantial, but the effort sent waves of agony through his remaining consciousness. He was aware of Lunar's shadow energy supporting his own, providing a stable framework around which his twilight essence could gather.

"His cohesion is failing," Lunar stated. "He requires energy replenishment."

Eclipse felt himself being moved to a low cot in the corner of the cabin. Through fragmenting awareness, he registered Poppy drawing heavy curtains over the windows, plunging the room into near-darkness save for a single lamp with a purple scarf draped over it.

The diffused light created a twilight-like atmosphere, not the same as his home zone, but reminiscent enough that Eclipse felt his essence responding. Lunar continued to provide shadow support, his own energy carefully regulated to avoid overwhelming Eclipse's weakened state.

Rowan knelt beside Eclipse. "What are we going to do?

"After you left, Galaxy Brides contacted Lunar again," Poppy explained. "They said they would pick us up for an emergency extraction. Soon."

Eclipse struggled to process what was happening. His fragmented consciousness recalled something vital he'd overheard during his captivity at Milano.

"Communication... intercepted..."

He tried to form the words, to warn them, but his essence scattered with the effort. Rowan reached for him, her hand passing through his form before finding a more solid region near what would be his core.

"He's trying to tell us something," she said, her connection with him still active enough to sense his distress. "Something about communications."

Eclipse gathered what remained of his strength, focusing on the memory of what he'd heard during brief moments of clarity at the Milano facility.

"Milano intercepted... Galaxy Brides signal..."

The words formed weakly in their shared consciousness, but Rowan understood.

"Milano intercepted Galaxy Brides' communications," she translated for the others. "They know about the extraction point."

Lunar darkened, absorbing more light from the room. "That must be why Gary changed their fourteen-day plan."

"We were supposed to have more time," Poppy whispered.

"When we were training for Earth on the ship, Galaxy Brides mentioned a possible emergency protocol if Earth threats discovered our location." Lunar's shadow essence shifted uncomfortably. "They deliberately kept details vague in case one of us was compromised."

Eclipse managed to stabilize his form enough to project a clearer thought to Rowan.

"Heard Milano scientists... discussing intercepted transmission... about planetary alignment tonight... creating extraction window..."

"Tonight?" Rowan's voice cracked. "You're leaving tonight?"

Lunar frowned, his shadow essence rippling with the motion. He stared at Eclipse as if he could also hear his friend's thoughts. "Milano's pursuit has forced Galaxy Brides to accelerate their timeline. They cannot risk waiting."

Eclipse felt Rowan's emotions surge through their connection. Shock turned to confusion, and a sharp pain as the realization that their time was ending far sooner than expected.

"But—" she began, then stopped as the distant sound of helicopter rotors grew louder.

Poppy moved to the window, carefully peering through a gap in the curtains. "I count three helicopters circling the area."

Eclipse attempted to rise and prepare for defense, but his essence scattered with the effort. Rowan placed her hand where his shoulder would be, somehow finding the right place despite his unstable form.

"Don't," she whispered. "Save your strength."

Lunar moved to the center of the cabin, his shadow essence extending to inspect the shielding. "The protection remains intact. Milano's scanners cannot penetrate the mineral composition of the roof. As long as we're careful, they won't find us."

Eclipse relaxed slightly, allowing his twilight energy to focus on regeneration rather than defense. The cabin's artificial twilight helped, providing an environment more conducive to his recovery than the harsh desert sun or complete darkness would have been.

As his essence gradually stabilized, memories of his captivity surfaced. He remembered the tests, the pain, Director Vega's cold assessment of his value as a research subject. But more disturbing were the fragments of information he'd gathered during moments of semi-consciousness.

"Must tell them... what I learned..."

Rowan sensed his intention. "You need to rest first. Recover some strength."

"No time... Milano knows... about Zorveya..."

This caught Lunar's attention. His shadow form consolidated near Eclipse's cot. "Explain."

With Rowan's help in translating his fragmented thoughts, Eclipse revealed what he'd overheard. Milano had encountered other alien species before, including Bevlonians. They had been developing technology based on these encounters, preparing for what Vega referred to as the inevitable expansion.

"They don't just want to study us," Rowan summarized. "They want to weaponize alien technology. Prepare Earth for some kind of interstellar conflict."

"Typical primitive species paranoia," Lunar commented, though his tone lacked its usual dismissiveness.

"Is it paranoia if there really are hostile aliens?" Poppy asked from her position by the window.

Eclipse struggled to organize his thoughts, to convey the most critical information.

"They know... extraction coordinates... tonight... trap..."

"Eclipse says Milano knows where the extraction is happening tonight," Rowan translated. "He thinks they're setting a trap."

Lunar's shadow essence darkened further. "This complicates matters. Galaxy Brides cannot be notified. Any transmission might be intercepted."

"So what do we do?" Poppy asked. "We can't just walk into an ambush, but we can't miss the extraction either."

Eclipse felt a strange calm settling over him as the situation clarified. His diplomatic training had prepared him for moments like this.

"Alternative extraction point..."

The thought formed more coherently as his essence continued to stabilize. Rowan looked at him questioningly.

"You know another location?" she asked.

Eclipse focused, gathering his strength to communicate more directly.

"Emergency protocol... in case of compromise... the original landing site..."

"The crash site," Lunar realized. "Where we first arrived. It's hardly logical from a strategic point of view, but it would be something Bob and Gary would think of."

"But that's miles from here," Poppy objected. "And Milano probably has that area under surveillance, too."

"Distraction needed... divide forces..."

Eclipse's form wavered as fatigue threatened to overwhelm him again. Rowan's hand found the most substantial part of his essence, her touch somehow anchoring him.

"Rest now," she said softly. "We'll figure out the details."

Eclipse allowed himself to drift into a recovery state, his twilight essence slowly regenerating in the artificial dusk of the cabin. The conversation continued around him, Lunar and the others discussing options, but Eclipse's awareness faded in and out.

In this semi-conscious state, time lost its meaning. He existed in a liminal space between alertness and oblivion, aware only of Rowan's presence beside him, her energy signature a constant that guided his recovery.

When he next achieved full consciousness, the cabin was darker, and Rowan was asleep, her head resting on her arms at the edge of his cot. His twilight form had stabilized significantly, though still far from his full strength.

Lunar materialized from the shadows in the corner.

"You recover quickly for one so damaged," he observed quietly.

Eclipse gathered his essence into a more defined shape, enough to communicate without disturbing Rowan.

"How long do we have?"

"Four hours," Lunar replied. "The extraction window opens in three more."

Eclipse looked down at Rowan's sleeping form, her face peaceful despite the crisis surrounding them. The choice loomed before him. He could return to Zorveya as planned, fulfilling the mission parameters, or remain on Earth with Rowan.

"Milano still searching?"

Lunar nodded. "They maintain a perimeter, but have not yet detected this location. Poppy is monitoring their communications." He gestured to where

Poppy sat by a small radio, headphones covering her ears.

Eclipse carefully extended his consciousness, testing the limits of his recovered strength. He was functional, though far from his full capacity. He was strong enough to travel, at least.

"The plan if Harris does not come for us?"

"Diversion at the original extraction coordinates," Lunar explained. "Poppy will trigger remote devices to simulate energy signatures. Meanwhile, we proceed to the crash site for true extraction."

It was a sound strategy, though risky. Eclipse considered the variables, the potential outcomes, and the likelihood of success.

"And if we miss the extraction?"

Lunar's shadow essence rippled, the equivalent of a shrug. "I calculate that Galaxy Alien Mail Order Brides will not want to return for at least another full planetary cycle. They will want to make sure that the danger has passed. Approximately one Earth year."

The implications settled over Eclipse. A year on Earth. A year with Rowan. The thought created a resonance he couldn't entirely suppress.

"You will go?"

Lunar was silent for a long moment. "I have fulfilled the mission parameters. Demonstrated cooperation with opposing factions. Made connections with Earth entities." His shadow form shifted, condensing slightly. "But Poppy wishes to remain on Earth."

Eclipse understood the unstated conflict. Lunar had formed his own attachment, just as Solar had with Dani. The mission had succeeded in ways none of them had anticipated.

"The council will be displeased."

"The council expected failure," Lunar countered. "Our success disrupts their political calculations."

Lunar was right, of course. There was no denying the truth. The mission had been designed as exile, a way to remove influential voices from Zorveya's increasingly polarized political landscape. By succeeding where failure was expected, they had created a diplomatic complication.

Rowan stirred beside him, her eyes opening slowly. When she saw his more coherent form, relief washed over her face.

"You're better," she said, reaching out to touch his now-solid shoulder.

"Recovering," he confirmed, their connection allowing direct communication.

Rowan smiled, though it didn't reach her eyes.

"Good. We're going to need you at full strength for tonight."

Eclipse sensed the conflict within her. She felt joy at his recovery, but it was mixed with dread at their imminent separation.

He found his voice, and started to say, "Rowan, I—"

A sharp knock at the door interrupted him. Poppy pulled off her headphones, eyes wide with alarm. Lunar's shadow form immediately expanded, preparing for defense.

"Galaxy Alien Mail Order Brides," Lunar identified, moving toward the door.

Poppy held up a hand to stop him. "Wait. How do you know it's Galaxy Brides? We should be careful. It could be a trap."

"I don't think Milano would knock on the door," Rowan countered.

Eclipse gathered his strength, preparing to defend them if necessary. His essence was still fragile, but he would not allow harm to come to Rowan or the others.

Lunar approached the door cautiously, his shadow essence extending to sense what lay beyond. After a moment, he nodded. "It is Galaxy Brides."

He opened the door to reveal a single figure.

"Harris?" Eclipse recognized the trainee who had piloted their ship during the crash landing. The smaller yellow alien wore what appeared to be a partially scorched Earth business suit.

"Emergency extraction protocol enacted," Harris announced, his translator functioning properly for once. "Location discovered. Milano forces are converging. Must depart immediately."

Rowan rose to her feet. "I thought the extraction wasn't until later. We were supposed to have more time."

"Emergency backup plan activated. Primary extraction compromised. Milano knows all contingencies," Harris said, his huge eyes blinking rapidly. "Bob and Gary detected the Milano communication pattern. They prepare an ambush at both primary and secondary locations. And three backup locations. Also, the place we like to order pizza from."

Eclipse exchanged glances with Lunar.

"Transport waiting one kilometer north. Must hurry," Harris said.

Eclipse gathered his essence, preparing to move, but a wave of weakness washed over him. He was still far from his full strength.

Rowan steadied him, her hand finding the most solid part of his form. "Can you make it?"

"Yes. With help."

"I've got you," she promised, supporting him as he struggled to maintain cohesion.

Poppy quickly gathered supplies while Lunar conferred with Harris about the extraction details. Eclipse focused on conserving his strength for the journey ahead.

As they prepared to leave, he became acutely aware that these might be his final moments on Earth with Rowan. The thought created discord in his energy patterns. This was not how he wanted their time together to end.

16

THE EXTRACTION POINT WAS NOTHING MORE than a small clearing in the desert, unremarkable except for a cluster of unusual rock formations that reminded Eclipse of the crystalline structures in the Twilight Belt back home. As Harris led them toward it, the first hints of dawn colored the eastern sky. It felt like appropriate timing for a diplomat perpetually caught between light and darkness.

"Coordinates match," Harris confirmed, his enormous eyes scanning the surroundings. "Extraction window opens in seventeen Earth minutes. Give or take."

Eclipse moved carefully, conserving his still-depleted energy. The journey from the cabin had been arduous, forcing them to take a circuitous route to avoid Milano's search patterns. Rowan remained close by his side, her occasional touch helping to stabilize his fluctuating form.

"So this is it," she said softly, looking around the clearing. "Just wait for the spaceship and... what? They beam you up?"

Her attempt at humor didn't mask the pain in her voice. Eclipse felt it resonating through their connection, mirroring his own internal discord.

"What is this beam up?" he asked.

"Doesn't matter," she whispered.

"*Galaxy Brides uses dimensional fold technology. The extraction creates a temporary bridge between spatial coordinates,*" he explained, his thoughts flowing directly to her.

"Like a wormhole?"

"*Similar, though less stable.*"

Lunar moved silently around the perimeter, his shadow essence extended to detect any approaching threats. Poppy followed a few steps behind, her expression unreadable in the dim light.

"Milano is expanding their search grid. We have perhaps thirty minutes before they reach this sector," Lunar reported.

Harris fidgeted nervously, checking and rechecking a small device that resembled a pocket watch. "Thirteen minutes to the extraction window. All must be ready."

Eclipse sensed Rowan's increasing tension. Her energy signature pulsed with anxiety, grief, and a determination that puzzled him. What was she planning?

"Rowan," he projected gently. *"We must discuss—"*

"No," she cut him off, stepping away slightly. "Let's not do the goodbye speech yet, okay? They're not even here. We have time." A tear slipped over her cheek. "We were supposed to have more time."

Eclipse wanted to respect her wish, though the words he needed to say pressed against his consciousness. *"Rowan, I—"*

Lunar approached with purpose. "I require a moment of your attention, Eclipse."

His shadow form had condensed into its most humanoid appearance.

Eclipse inclined his head in acknowledgment.

"I have completed an analysis of our mission parameters and outcomes," Lunar began. "The experiment was designed to prove that opposing forces could coexist harmoniously when removed from their natural environment and given a common purpose."

"That is correct," Eclipse confirmed what they both already knew.

Eclipse waited, sensing there was more to Lunar's statement than a mission summary.

"However," Lunar continued, his shadow essence rippling slightly, "I have reached an unexpected conclusion. The connection formed with my Earth counterpart has created a harmonious resonance that exceeds mission parameters."

Eclipse felt a surge of surprise. For Lunar to speak so openly about his feelings for Poppy was unprecedented. The shadow-dwellers of the Lunaris Zone were known for their emotional reserve.

"What I mean to say," Lunar struggled uncharacteristically with his words, "is that I wish to remain on Earth."

The declaration hung in the air between them. Harris made a small choking sound.

"Not possible," the Galaxy Brides representative protested. "Extraction coordinates programmed for three entities. Eclipse, Lunar, Harris."

"Then reprogram for two," Lunar replied coolly. "I have made my choice."

Eclipse studied his companion, sensing the resolution in his energy pattern. This was no impulsive decision.

"The council will consider this abandonment of duty," Eclipse warned.

"Yes," Lunar agreed simply. "They will."

"They may declare you exiled permanently."

"I am aware."

Poppy had moved closer during this exchange, her hand hovering near but not quite touching Lunar's shadow form.

"Are you sure about this?" she asked softly. "Your home—"

"Will never accept my true nature," Lunar completed. "Here, in darkness and in light, I am myself."

Eclipse felt a resonance with Lunar's words that shook him to his core. How many cycles had he spent in the Twilight Belt, never fully belonging to either light or shadow? Always mediating, never simply being.

Harris' device emitted a series of urgent beeps. "Seven minutes to extraction window. Must prepare."

The Galaxy Brides trainee scurried about the clearing, setting up small devices at specific intervals. Eclipse recognized the pattern. They would form the dimensional coordinates for the extraction field.

Rowan moved to Eclipse's side again, her energy brushing against his.

"So Lunar's staying," she said quietly. "What about you?"

Before Eclipse could respond, a distant sound caught their attention. The distinctive thump of helicopter rotors carried across the desert.

"Milano," Lunar confirmed, his shadow essence extending to scan the horizon. "Multiple aerial vehicles approaching from the southwest. Ground transport following."

Harris squeaked in alarm. "Four minutes to extraction. Not enough time to relocate!"

Eclipse assessed their situation with the clarity of a diplomat accustomed to crisis. Milano would arrive just as the extraction window opened. They would have seconds, not minutes, to make their departure.

And he still hadn't discussed his feelings with Rowan.

"We need to mask our position," Poppy said, panicked. "We need something to slow them down."

Lunar nodded. "I will create a diversion. My shadow-walking abilities allow me to move undetected."

"No," Poppy protested. "It's too dangerous."

"I am most suited to the task," Lunar insisted. "I have chosen this planet. I must begin defending it."

"Three minutes!" Harris wailed.

The helicopter sounds grew louder. Searchlights swept the desert floor in the distance, methodically closing in on their position.

Eclipse felt a surge of respect for his formerly antagonistic companion. Lunar had always been the most reserved of their trio, the least likely to take risks. Yet here he stood, volunteering for danger.

As Lunar prepared to depart, Harris suddenly let out a distressed chirp. The small devices he'd been arranging began to flicker erratically.

"Problem. Big problem," he exclaimed, his enormous eyes widening even further. "Extraction field unstable. Energy matrix destabilizing!"

Eclipse moved toward the devices, his twilight essence reaching out to sense the dimensional calculations. Immediately, he detected the flaw. The extraction field was calibrated for three specific energy signatures—his own twilight form, Solar's light energy, and Lunar's shadow essence. With Solar already extracted and his own energy severely weakened, the field lacked the necessary balance. It could not carry three different signatures. It would need to be stabilized.

Harris didn't understand the technology he was implementing. It would never work like this.

"What's happening?" Rowan asked, looking between Harris and Eclipse.

"The dimensional bridge requires balanced energy to form properly," Eclipse explained. "Without Solar, and with my essence depleted, the bridge is going to collapse, and it will take the ship waiting for us with it."

Rowan looked up at the sky in worry. "Dani and Solar are up there. Are you saying their ship will explode or something?"

The helicopter sounds were alarmingly close now.

Eclipse turned to Rowan, knowing it was time. The words he needed to say could no longer wait.

"Rowan," he began, gathering his twilight essence into its most coherent form. "There is something I must tell you."

She looked up at him, her eyes reflecting the blue glow of the extraction devices.

"I know what you're going to say," she said, her voice tight with emotion. "You have to go back. You have a duty to your people. You need to warn them about Milano. I understand."

Eclipse reached out, his twilight essence brushing against her cheek in the closest approximation of a human caress he could manage.

"That is not what I was going to say."

Searchlights swept over the nearby ridge. Any moment now, Milano's forces would spot them.

Eclipse tried to expand his energy field to stop it and instantly retracted in pain.

"Stop, you're not strong enough," Lunar told him. He stepped forward, his shadow form extending toward one of the flickering devices. "I can stabilize it with my shadow energy. I'll have to go up."

"But you wanted to stay," Eclipse said, sensing Lunar's regret.

"As do you if given the choice," Lunar replied, his shadow essence rippling with resignation. "But one of us must go. Your essence is too depleted for the journey. The council needs to know about Milano's technology."

"Can't Harris adjust it?" Poppy asked desperately, the realization dawning on her face.

Harris shook his head vigorously. "No. No. No."

"Pull yourself together," Rowan ordered.

"Field parameters set by Bob and Gary," Harris muttered. "Need specific energy triangle. Light, shadow, twilight."

The alien frantically ran around to adjust controls that clearly made no difference before tripping and falling face-first onto the rocky ground.

"Is he...?" Rowan began.

Harris pushed himself up and held his head. Miserably, he said, "Pudding."

"He's fine," Lunar dismissed.

Lunar stood motionless, his shadow form contracting slightly. Eclipse could sense the conflict within him. His desire to remain with Poppy clashed with the harsh reality of their situation.

Harris stumbled in circles, holding his head.

"If one of us doesn't control the energy, the ship will be lost," Lunar was saying to Poppy. "Solar, Dani, all those aboard, will die."

"Can't Harris...?" Poppy tried to argue.

"Someone needs to return with Solar. My people will not trust him if he's alone," Lunar said.

Poppy shook her head, as if she could push away what he was telling her.

"Galaxy Brides cannot be trusted to deliver critical intelligence," Lunar said, his voice hardening. "The council will dismiss any such message without verification from an authorized entity."

Poppy moved closer to him. "You're saying you have to go."

"Yes." The single word carried the weight of resignation and duty.

The helicopter sounds grew dangerously close now.

"Pudding!" Harris shrieked, diving toward the center of the array.

"Eclipse," Lunar said, turning to him, "you must remain. Your twilight energy is too weak for the extraction. And Milano has already studied your energy patterns. They can't learn more from you that will harm our people. But if they were to find Solar or I..."

Eclipse nodded, not needing him to finish the thought. "If you go back, the council may not permit your return."

"You have beaten Milano once," Lunar said, ignoring the warning. "You are best equipped to evade them."

Eclipse understood the unspoken truth. Lunar was making his own sacrifice, choosing duty over his personal desires, so that Eclipse didn't have to.

"The threat must be communicated properly," Eclipse said. "The weapons they have developed, their knowledge of our physiology, and their intentions toward interstellar expansion. These represent a potential danger to Zorveya in the not so distant future."

Lunar moved closer to Eclipse, his shadow

essence condensing to its most focused form. "Promise me you will protect Poppy," he said, his voice low enough that only Eclipse could hear. "Until I return."

Eclipse's twilight essence pulsed with solemn agreement. "I promise. For as long as it takes."

"And tell her..." Lunar hesitated. "Tell her everything I could not."

Eclipse nodded.

Lunar pulled Poppy aside. Eclipse gave them space as he turned to Rowan.

"Pudding," Harris said in a panic.

The Milano helicopter crested the ridge, its spotlight sweeping across the clearing.

Lunar's shadow essence was now fully focused and controlled. He turned to Eclipse, rippling with unusual emotion. "It has been educational serving with you, Diplomat Eclipse."

"And with you, Intelligence Specialist Lunar. Tell the council what happened here. Tell them Earth has potential beyond their imagining. And tell them I have found my true function at last," Eclipse said.

Lunar's form shifted, becoming almost invisible as he merged with the pre-dawn shadows.

"Protect her," he said to Eclipse, gesturing toward Poppy before he vanished into the darkness.

Poppy reached out as Lunar faded from view, her hand passing through the last wisps of his shadow essence. Eclipse felt her grief resonating across the clearing, a pain so sharp it momentarily disrupted his own energy patterns.

"He will return," Eclipse told her, though he could not be certain it was true.

Rowan moved to Poppy's side, putting an arm around her shoulders.

"Come with us," she said firmly. "You're not staying here for Milano to find."

Poppy nodded numbly, her eyes still fixed on the spot where Lunar had vanished.

The extraction devices began to hum, emitting a soft blue glow as they activated. Harris bustled between them.

Rowan furrowed her brow in annoyance.

Eclipse took Rowan's hands in his, his twilight form stabilizing at the points of contact. Their energies resonated together, creating that perfect harmonic convergence he had never experienced before her.

"I choose Earth," he said simply. "I choose you. I'm staying."

Rowan's eyes widened. "But your mission—"

"Lunar will deliver the report. The council will receive the necessary information about Milano's threat."

"But your home—"

He thought about how he tried to leave his post as an ambassador, and his people sent him here. It was hard not to think of that as a punishment. "There, I am always in between. It is not where I belong. Not anymore. Here, with you, I have found something I did not know was possible."

A helicopter's spotlight found them in the clearing. Voices shouted commands as Milano forces spotted the extraction array.

Harris yelled frantic nonsense.

Eclipse continued, knowing their time was precious. "On Zorveya, I was defined by function. Eclipse the Diplomat. The Mediator. Here, I am simply Eclipse. And with you, I am more than I ever thought possible."

Tears formed in Rowan's eyes. "Are you sure? This isn't just some quantum harmonic thing making you feel this way?"

Eclipse's twilight essence brightened. "The resonance between us is real, but my choice is made with full awareness. The Earth words are hardly adequate, but I love you, Rowan Clark. A concept my kind rarely expresses, but one I have come to understand through you."

"I love you, too," she whispered.

The extraction devices reached full power, creating a shimmering field in the center of the array. Harris stood within it, his form already beginning to blur.

Milano vehicles screeched to a halt at the edge of the clearing. Armed personnel poured out, Director Vega at their head.

"Secure the aliens," Vega ordered. "Don't let them escape!"

The extraction field intensified, the air within it seeming to fold in impossible directions.

Eclipse pulled Rowan and Poppy away from the array, his twilight essence expanding to shield them as the first energy pulses from Milano's weapons streaked toward them. He gathered his strength for one final effort. His twilight essence expanded outward in all directions, creating a dome of purple-blue energy around the three of them. The Milano weapons fired, their pulses glancing across his field but failing to penetrate.

Through their connection, Rowan felt his plan. "Eclipse, you're not strong enough yet!"

"Together, we are," he replied, drawing on their resonance to reinforce his fading strength.

In a flash of brilliant light, the extraction field collapsed in on itself. Harris vanished, leaving only a shimmering distortion that quickly faded.

Eclipse used the extraction field's collapse as a cover to get away.

"No," Vega shouted, running forward. "Secure the remaining entities!"

With a sound like thunder, Eclipse's field pulsed outward in a concussive wave. The Milano forces were thrown back, their weapons scattered. In the momentary chaos, Eclipse condensed his essence around Rowan and Poppy and surged away from the clearing, flowing like liquid twilight between the rocks.

They had perhaps minutes before pursuit would reorganize. Minutes to disappear into the vastness of the desert. Minutes to begin their new life together.

As they fled, Eclipse was acutely aware of both women's energy signatures. Rowan's familiar warmth resonated with his own essence. But Poppy's felt more like grief-tinged determination. He had made a promise to Lunar, one he intended to keep.

As they fled into the growing light of dawn,

Eclipse felt something he had never truly experienced in all his cycles as a diplomat on Zorveya.

Freedom.

"I don't know what comes next," he admitted to Rowan as they sprinted across the desert floor.

She smiled, her hand intertwined with his twilight essence. "Neither do I. But we'll figure it out together."

Poppy, running alongside them, glanced back toward the clearing where Lunar had disappeared into the extraction field.

"All of us," Rowan said softly. "We'll figure it out together."

For a being who had existed in the perpetual in-between, in the balance point of opposing forces, that simple certainty was the most profound gift of all.

CHAPTER 17

EPILOGUE

Rowan woke to the sensation of gentle vibrations against her skin. Eclipse was watching her again, his twilight essence stretched out beside her on the bed, stars swimming in his eyes. In the months since they'd escaped Milano, she'd grown accustomed to waking this way, wrapped in the subtle hum of his energy, the morning light filtering through the curtains of their small rented cabin creating the perfect twilight conditions he thrived in.

"You're staring," she murmured, smiling without opening her eyes fully.

"Observing," he corrected, the familiar response now part of their morning ritual. "Your biorhythms align perfectly with the Earth's sunrise cycles."

Rowan laughed softly. Even in love, Eclipse

couldn't help analyzing everything. It was endearing how he tried to understand human experiences through his scientific perspective.

"Normal people just say good morning," she told him, finally opening her eyes to take in his twilight form. In private, he never bothered with the human disguise. Here, he could simply be himself, a swirling galaxy of purple-blue energy that somehow managed to look at her with more adoration than any human ever had.

"Good morning," he conceded, his essence rippling with amusement. "Poppy has already departed for her supply run."

Rowan nodded, stretching as she sat up. Their little cabin, tucked away in a remote corner of the Coconino National Forest, had become their sanctu-ary. Technically, it was an old ranger outpost, but Pete knew a guy who knew a gal and hooked them up with it. Far from Duskrock and Milano's search parties, they'd created something resembling a normal life, if normal included hiding an alien diplomat and helping another alien's heartbroken girlfriend monitor deep space frequencies for messages.

"Did she sleep at all?" Rowan asked, concerned about their housemate. Poppy spent most nights at the makeshift communications array she'd built, listening for any signal that might be from Lunar.

"Two hours, forty-three minutes," Eclipse reported. "An improvement over previous nights."

Rowan sighed, swinging her legs over the side of the bed. "She's going to make herself sick."

"Her dedication is admirable," Eclipse noted, "if physiologically inadvisable."

"Says the alien who doesn't need sleep," Rowan teased, pulling on a robe and heading toward the bathroom.

When she emerged, Eclipse had assumed his more humanoid form, though still composed entirely of twilight energy. They'd discovered he could maintain this shape with minimal effort, allowing him to interact with objects in the human world more easily without the restrictions of the skin-suit.

Rowan made coffee while Eclipse prepared a simple breakfast. It had taken some trial and error to teach him human cooking. His first attempt at toast had ended with a minor kitchen fire when he'd tried to calculate the optimal molecular vibration frequency—*or some such nonsense*—instead of using the toaster... but he'd proven to be a quick study.

"The Milano search patterns have shifted again,"

Eclipse informed her as they ate. "Their primary focus appears to have returned to Duskrock."

Rowan nodded, processing this information. They monitored Milano's movements through careful checks of online news sources and the encrypted communications channel Pete occasionally used to update them.

"Do you think they've given up looking for us?" she asked.

"Not entirely," Eclipse replied thoughtfully. "But their resources are finite. They cannot maintain high-intensity pursuit indefinitely. They should eventually conclude that we all went home."

Rowan sipped her coffee, watching Eclipse's twilight form shimmer in the morning sunlight streaming through the kitchen window. Sometimes it still struck her as surreal, sitting in a cabin kitchen having breakfast with an alien from another world who had chosen her over his home planet.

"Any regrets?" she asked suddenly, the question escaping before she could reconsider.

Eclipse's form stilled, his starlit eyes focusing on her with that intensity that always made her heart skip. "About choosing Earth? About choosing you?"

Rowan nodded, trying to keep her expression neutral despite the flutter of uncertainty in her chest.

"None," he stated simply. His twilight essence expanded slightly, reaching across the table to envelop her free hand in warmth. "The council would not have listened to me any more closely than Solar or Lunar. They would have assigned me to another diplomatic post where I would once again serve as mediator between forces with no desire for reconciliation."

He paused, his essence shifting into patterns she'd come to recognize as deep contemplation.

"Here, I have purpose beyond function. I have connection beyond duty." His form brightened as he added, "I have you."

The simple declaration melted away her momentary insecurity. Rowan smiled, turning her hand to intertwine her fingers with his twilight essence. The familiar harmonic resonance hummed between them, creating that perfect sense of belonging she'd never experienced before meeting him.

"Besides," Eclipse continued, a hint of amusement in his energy patterns, "I am not entirely without function here. Helping Poppy construct her communication array has allowed me to apply considerable theoretical knowledge."

Rowan laughed. "You're such a nerd. An alien diplomat nerd."

"I am unfamiliar with this nerd designation," Eclipse replied, though his essence rippled in what she recognized as his version of laughter.

The sound of tires on gravel announced Poppy's return. Moments later, the cabin door opened, and Poppy entered carrying several bags of supplies. Her appearance had improved since those first difficult weeks after Lunar's departure. The dark circles under her eyes had faded somewhat, and her movements had regained some of their former vitality. Rowan wasn't fooled, though. Poppy was struggling without Lunar.

"Morning," Poppy called, setting the bags on the counter. "The general store had actual fresh vegetables today. I nearly wept."

Rowan rose to help unpack. "Any news from town?"

Poppy's expression brightened slightly. "Actually, yes. I ran into Pete. "

"Oh?" Rowan asked, surprised.

"Apparently, after the police questioned him for the unlawful alien parade he hosted, he's been playing up the whole I-was-abducted-by-the-government angle. It's been great for business." Poppy pulled out a newspaper and laid it on the table. "But here's the interesting part."

The front page featured a blurry photograph of what appeared to be a Milano facility, with the headline, *"Tech Company Denies Government Contracts for Weapons Research."*

Rowan scanned the article quickly. "Someone's investigating them."

"The reporter's name seemed familiar," Poppy said. "I thought maybe you'd know them?"

Rowan looked at the byline and felt a jolt of recognition. "Michaels. He was my mentor at the Phoenix paper." She looked up at Eclipse, excitement building. "This is perfect. He always believed my stories about Milano. If we could get our evidence to him—"

"It would be extremely dangerous," Eclipse cautioned, his twilight form condensing slightly with concern.

"But worth considering," Poppy added. "Milano's been operating in the shadows for too long. If enough light gets shined on them..."

Rowan nodded, her journalistic instincts awakening after months of lying low. Excitement filled her. "We'd need to be careful. Anonymous drops, encrypted communications."

"We should discuss this thoroughly before taking action," Eclipse said, his diplomat's caution evident.

"Of course," Rowan agreed, reaching out to touch his twilight essence reassuringly. "We make decisions together, remember?"

His form brightened at her words, and Rowan felt that now-familiar surge of connection between them.

Poppy excused herself to check on her communication array, leaving them alone in the kitchen.

"You miss it," Eclipse observed once she'd gone. "Your function as a truth-seeker."

Rowan considered his words.

"I do," she admitted. "Being a journalist was more than just a job. It was about exposing what needed to be exposed, helping people understand what was happening in the world."

"Perhaps there is a way for you to resume this function while maintaining our security," Eclipse suggested. "A balanced approach."

His words reminded her of why she'd fallen for him in the first place. He had an ability to see multiple perspectives, to find harmony in seemingly conflicting goals.

"Maybe there is," she agreed. "We'll figure it out."

Eclipse's twilight form shifted closer to her, enveloping her in gentle warmth. "Together."

Rowan leaned into his embrace, marveling at

how natural it felt to be held by a being made of twilight energy. If someone had told her six months ago that she'd fall in love with an alien diplomat who existed in a state between light and shadow, she would have laughed them out of the room.

Yet here she was, completely at home in his otherworldly embrace.

Outside, the morning sun climbed higher in the sky, casting long shadows across the forest floor. Inside their small cabin, the light filtering through the curtains created the perfect balance of illumination, not too bright, not too dark. Twilight.

Rowan smiled at the symbolism. They existed in their own twilight zone, neither fully part of Eclipse's world nor entirely of Earth's. Creating something new in the space between.

"What are you thinking?" Eclipse asked, sensing her contemplative mood.

"That I never expected to find home in the in-between," she answered truthfully.

Eclipse's essence brightened with understanding. "The balance point has always been my place, but never before has it felt like where I truly belong."

Before Rowan could respond, a sudden commotion came from Poppy's room as equipment crashed onto the floor, and she gave a startled exclamation.

They rushed to investigate, finding Poppy staring wide-eyed at her communication array, which was emitting a series of distinct pulses.

"It's a signal," she whispered, hands trembling as she adjusted dials. "A pattern. Three short, three long, three short."

"S.O.S.," Rowan translated.

Eclipse moved closer to the equipment, his twilight essence extending to sense the energy patterns.

"The frequency matches Zorveyan communication protocols," he confirmed. "But there is something else embedded within it."

The signal shifted, resolving into a voice transmission so distorted by distance and interference that it was barely recognizable. But one word came through clearly, "Coming."

Poppy's eyes filled with tears as she clutched the receiver. "Lunar?" She touched the device. "What does that mean? I don't understand. Lunar?"

Eclipse's twilight form pulsed with surprise and what Rowan recognized as hope.

Rowan put an arm around Poppy's shoulders as they all stared at the communication array. The message repeated once more before fading back into static.

In that moment, standing in their hideaway cabin with an alien she loved and a friend who had just received hope from across the stars, Rowan felt a certainty settle over her. Whatever came next, whether it was exposing Milano, helping Lunar return to Earth, or simply building their unusual life together, they would face it as they had everything else.

Together, in the perfect balance of twilight.

The End

THE SERIES

Galaxy Alien Mail Order Brides Series

Spark

Flame

Blaze

Ice

Frost

Snow

Eclipse Bound

Solar Bound

Lunar Bound

Solar Bound

Sci-fi Paranormal Romantic Comedy

He glows. She burns. Together, they're impossible to hide.

When Solar, a golden-skinned guard from the eternal daylight of Solarus, crash-lands outside Duskrock, Arizona, subtlety goes up in smoke. The catastrophically inept Galaxy Alien Mail Order Brides have blown his cover, UFO headlines are everywhere, and a black-ops outfit called Milano is already on the hunt. Then Solar meets Dani Ember, a fire dancer whose spark pulls him like gravity, and hiding becomes the last thing on his mind.

Dani has always trusted flame more than people until an alien warrior explodes into her life, glowing like sunlight made flesh. Forced into hiding together, their connection ignites hotter with every touch. But with aliens Eclipse and Lunar also in Milano's crosshairs, duty and desire collide. To save his companions, protect Earth, and give his divided world a chance at peace, Solar must make the one choice he never planned for... claiming the human who feels like home.

--

SOLAR BOUND is a steamy sci-fi paranormal romantic comedy with a grumpy golden alien and a sunshine fire dancer, forced proximity on Earth, sizzling open-door heat, black-ops hunters, and a guaranteed HEA with no cliffhanger.

Book two of the Bound Trilogy installment from the Galaxy Alien Mail Order Brides series.

Updated Reading List and Links here:
MichellePillow.com

READING GUIDES

MICHELLE M. PILLOW NOVELS

Free Reading Guides

Download free reading guides at
MichellePillow.com.

ABOUT THE AUTHOR

New York Times & *USA TODAY*
Bestselling Author

Michelle loves to travel and try new things, whether it's a paranormal investigation of an old Vaudeville Theatre or climbing Mayan temples in Belize. She believes life is an adventure fueled by copious amounts of coffee.

Newly relocated to the American South, Michelle is involved in various film and documentary projects with her talented director husband. She is mom to a fantastic artist. And she's managed by a dog and cat who make sure she's meeting her deadlines.

For the most part she can be found wearing pajama pants and working in her office. There may or may not be dancing. It's all part of the creative process.

Come say hello! Michelle loves talking with readers on social media!

www.MichellePillow.com

- facebook.com/AuthorMichellePillow
- x.com/michellepillow
- instagram.com/michellempillow
- bookbub.com/authors/michelle-m-pillow
- goodreads.com/Michelle_Pillow
- amazon.com/author/michellepillow
- youtube.com/michellepillow
- pinterest.com/michellepillow

PILLOW FIGHTER FAN CLUB!

FAN OF MICHELLE M. PILLOW?

Want to join an awesome group of readers?
facebook.com/groups/MichellePillowFanClub

THANK YOU FOR READING!

Please Leave a Review

Please take a moment to share your thoughts by reviewing this book.

Be sure to check out Michelle's other titles at www.MichellePillow.com

Imprint

The Raven Books LLC
1723 University Ave Suite B #247
Oxford MS 38655
United States

Telephone Number: 1 (662) 484-4174
Email: theravenbooks@gmail.com
CEO: Michelle M. Pillow
Website: michellepillow.com